“T
daughter would make me an ideal wife.”

“And so she would!” his mother agreed, not reluctant to add her voice to those that in recent weeks had urged the personable Lord Exmouth to seriously consider taking the matrimonial plunge once again. “She is without doubt the sweetest-natured girl you could ever wish to meet.”

“I wouldn’t argue with that,” he agreed amicably.

“She is compliant and delightful. She would never interfere with your pleasure, or cause you the least concern.”

“I should wish to know her a little better before voicing an opinion on certain aspects of her character. I strongly suspect that Miss Robina Percival possesses rather more spirit than most people realize.”

Lord Exmouth's Intentions

Anne Ashley

HARLEQUIN®

TORONTO • NEW YORK • LONDON
AMSTERDAM • PARIS • SYDNEY • HAMBURG
STOCKHOLM • ATHENS • TOKYO • MILAN • MADRID
PRAGUE • WARSAW • BUDAPEST • AUCKLAND

Special thanks and acknowledgment are given to Anne Ashley for her contribution to THE STEEPWOOD SCANDAL series.

ISBN 0-373-30424-2

LORD EXMOUTH'S INTENTIONS

First North American Publication 2003

This edition published by arrangement with Harlequin Books S.A.

Visit us at www.eHarlequin.com

Printed in U.S.A.

ANNE ASHLEY

was born and educated in Leicester. She lived for a time in Scotland, but now resides in the West Country with two cats, her two sons and a husband who has a wonderful and very necessary sense of humor. When not pounding away at the keys on her computer she likes to relax in her garden, which she has opened to the public on more than one occasion in aid of the village church funds.

THE STEEPWOOD SCANDAL:

Lord Ravensden's Marriage, by Anne Herries
An Innocent Miss, by Elizabeth Bailey
The Reluctant Bride, by Meg Alexander
A Companion of Quality, by Nicola Cornick
A Most Improper Proposal, by Gail Whitiker
A Noble Man, by Anne Ashley
An Unreasonable Match, by Sylvia Andrew
An Unconventional Duenna, by Paula Marshall
Counterfeit Earl, by Anne Herries
The Captain's Return, by Elizabeth Bailey
The Guardian's Dilemma, by Gail Whitiker
Lord Exmouth's Intentions, by Anne Ashley
Mr. Rushford's Honour, by Meg Alexander
An Unlikely Suitor, by Nicola Cornick
An Inescapable Match, by Sylvia Andrew
The Missing Marchioness, by Paula Marshall

Chapter One

A distinct lack of enthusiasm induced Robina to allow the half-folded garment to slip through her fingers, and her attention to wander aspeered through the window to follow the progress along the street of a very smart racing curricle, pulled by two superbly matched greys.

Considering the Season had officially come to an end the week before, London remained surprisingly bustling with life, its many springtime visitors seemingly reluctant to return to their country homes, or to move on to those coastal towns which had become such fashionable summer retreats in recent years.

It just so happened that she would have been more than happy to return to her Northamptonshire home, to sample once again the sweetly fresh country air, and be reunited with her father and sisters once more. She was not so foolish as to suppose that it would not take a little time to adjust to the tranquillity of the vicarage in Abbot Quincey again, after spending more than three months here in the capital, thoroughly enjoying all the delights of a Season which, even though she said so herself, had been something of a success.

For a simple country parson's daughter, with no dowry to speak of, she had managed to attract the attention of two very worthy gentlemen, either of whom, she didn't doubt for a moment, would have made a very considerate husband. She had been encouraged by her mother to turn down both offers for her hand, which she had dutifully done without, she hoped, causing lasting hurt to either erstwhile suitor. And certainly none whatsoever to herself!

Neither Mr Chard nor the Honourable Simon Sutherland had succeeded in igniting that illusive flame which every romantically inclined young woman longs to experience. She had come through what was likely to be her one and only London Season a little more worldly-wise and certainly heart-whole. An involuntary sigh escaped her. Whether or not she would be able to say the same by the end of the summer was a different matter entirely.

Without the least warning she experienced it yet again: that sudden surge of blind panic. Why, oh why, hadn't she flatly refused when the suggestion had first been put to her? Why had she allowed herself to be persuaded into accompanying the Dowager to Brighton, when she had in her heart of hearts known from the very first that what Lady Exmouth truly wanted was not a young companion for herself, but a biddable little wife for her son?

Abandoning the packing entirely now, Robina slumped down on the bed, not for the first time cursing herself for not being a little more assertive on occasions.

It wasn't that she had taken the Dowager's son in dislike. Nothing could have been further from the truth. Lord Exmouth was a very personable gentleman. If he was not quite the dashing, handsome hero of storybooks, he was certainly most attractive, blessed with a good physique and noble bearing. Just because he happened to be the wrong side of five-and-thirty was not such a drawback either, for older gentlemen, she had been reliably informed, tended to be rather more dependable.

That he rarely smiled, had more often than not a cynical glint in those very attractive dark brown eyes of his, and frequently relapsed into periods of brooding silence were traits, she didn't doubt, to which she would grow accustomed in time. What she knew she could never reconcile herself to, however, was always figuring as second best in the eyes of any man she agreed to marry. And that, she very much feared, would be precisely her fate if she was ever foolish enough to consent to a union with Lord Daniel Exmouth!

A sympathetic sigh escaped her this time as the many rumours concerning the very personable widower filtered through her mind. If half the stories circulating about him were true then the poor Baron was a mere shadow of his former self.

His heart, according to many, had died with his first wife in that tragic accident eighteen months ago. Many believed that, because he had been tooling the carriage when it had overturned, killing both his wife and the nephew of a near neighbour, the combination of both grief and guilt had changed him from the most companionable of gentlemen into a die-hard sceptic who now attained scant pleasure from life. Yet, for all his brooding glances and frequent periods of self-enforced solitude, he could still on occasions be both affable and charming. Sadly, that didn't alter the fact that whoever agreed to become his second wife would always live in the shadow of the beautiful Clarissa, who, many believed, had taken her husband's loving heart with her to her grave.

Her mother's unexpected appearance in the bedchamber put an end to these melancholy reflections, and Robina automatically rose to her feet to continue her packing.

'Great heavens, child! Haven't you finished yet? What on earth have you been doing all this time? You know full well that Lady Exmouth's servants will be here at noon to collect your trunk.'

Robina cast a glance in her mother's direction, not for the first time wishing that she were more able to assess her moods. The tone she had used had been mildly scolding, but her expression betrayed no hint of annoyance.

Would now be an appropriate moment to admit that she, too, would much prefer to return to Northamptonshire at the end of the week? Could she possibly succeed in making her mother, who was not always the most approachable of people, understand her grave misgivings about spending the summer in Brighton? Or had she foolishly left it rather too late?

'Mama, I have been having second thoughts about accompanying Lady Exmouth,' she said in a rush, before she could change her mind. 'I should much prefer to return with you to Abbot Quincey at the end of the week.'

The seconds ticked slowly by while Robina scanned her mother's face in the hope of glimpsing some visual reaction to the belated confession, but as usual Lady Elizabeth's expression remained as inscrutable as ever.

'Why this sudden change of heart, child?' Once again there was just the faintest hint of impatience in the beautifully cultured voice. 'Not so very long ago you were overjoyed at the prospect of spending the summer weeks by the sea. No pressure was brought to bear when the suggestion was first put to you. It was entirely your own decision to accept Lady Exmouth's very kind invitation.'

Robina could not argue with this. She had never made any secret of the fact that she had liked Lady Exmouth from the first moment they met, and the prospect of extending the period of frivolous enjoyment by spending several weeks as the guest of that delightful and highly sociable lady had been just too much of a temptation for the country parson's daughter, who had discovered that she had rapidly acquired a taste for the finer things in life. It was only when she had paid that short visit to Hampshire to be amongst the select few who attended the small party to celebrate the engagement of the Duke of Sharnbrook to Lady Sophia Cleeve that grave doubts had begun to assail her.

'In that case we shall not be seeing each other again until the autumn,' her good friend Sophia had remarked, after Robina had casually divulged her intention of spending the summer in Brighton as the guest of the Dowager Lady Exmouth.

They had been standing outside the glorious ducal mansion, bidding each other a final farewell, and there had been an unmistakable teasing glint in Sophia's eyes as she had added in an undertone, 'So, do I congratulate you now, or wait until the announcement is officially made, you sly old thing?'

Even now Robina could recall quite clearly gaping like a half-wit at her lifelong friend. 'I—I do not perfectly understand what you mean, Sophia. You are the one to be congratulated, not I.'

'At the moment, yes,' she had laughingly agreed, 'but it is quite obvious to anyone of the meanest intelligence that it will not be too long before you also are sporting a splendid betrothal ring on your left hand.'

Robina clearly recalled also her friend's teasing laughter before she had gone on to add rather tauntingly, 'Why, you cannot possibly go about refusing reasonable offers of marriage, while encouraging the attentions of a certain party, and happily accepting an invitation to spend the summer with that favoured gentleman's mother, without causing a deal of speculation. Surely you don't suppose that people haven't already put two and two together and realised that your affections are engaged! I have fallen desperately in love myself, and so am able to read the signs, my dear. But if you would prefer that I wait a little longer before offering my heartfelt congratulations, you only have to say so.'

Robina had been too stunned to say anything else at the time, and had been prey to the most guilt-ridden reflections and fearful conjecture ever since.

Had she in truth actively encouraged Lord Exmouth to suppose that a proposal of marriage from him would not be unwelcome? She had asked herself that selfsame question time and time again in recent days, and even now wasn't perfectly sure that she knew the answer.

She couldn't deny that, up until she and her mother had paid that short visit to Hampshire, she had not once refused to stand up with Lord Exmouth whenever they had happened to be attending the same party. Which, she now realised, had occurred far too frequently to have been mere coincidence. She could only marvel at how credulous she had been for supposing that pure chance had brought them together so often, and not, as she now strongly suspected, the designs of their respective mothers.

If her suspicions were correct then the Dowager believed that in the quiet and undemanding vicar's daughter she had found the ideal person to care for her two motherless granddaughters, and make the life of her heartbroken son more bearable, without demanding too much of him in return. It was also fairly safe to assume that her own mother was of a similar mind, and that she had every expectation of her eldest daughter receiving a very advantageous offer of marriage in the not too distant future.

'May I ask you something, Mama?' She did not wait for a response. 'Are you hoping that Lord Exmouth will make me an offer before the summer is over?'

Lady Elizabeth's expression remained inscrutable, and yet Robina sensed that her mother had been momentarily taken aback by the directness of the question. In truth, she had rather surprised herself that she had summoned up enough courage to ask such a thing. She was wont to treat her mother with the utmost respect as a rule, and had never been encouraged to query any decision she had chosen to make.

Evidently Lady Elizabeth did not deem the question an impertinence, for she said after a moment's quiet deliberation, 'I certainly believe he is not indifferent to you, Robina. And I cannot deny that, should he decide to make you an offer of marriage, I would be delighted, yes. It would be a truly splendid match, far better than I could ever have hoped for you. Carriages, jewels, fine clothes would be yours for the asking. You would want for nothing, child.'

Nothing except love, Robina longed to retort, but remained silent as she watched her mother move in that graceful way of hers across to the window.

'You must appreciate of course that if you did marry Exmouth, your sisters' chances of finding suitable husbands would be vastly improved. By reminding you of this, I hope you realise that I would never expect you to forfeit your own happiness in order that your sisters might attain theirs. Nothing could be further from the truth! And if I thought that your feelings were already engaged, I would not suggest for a moment that you further your acquaintance with the widower... But your affections are not engaged, are they, Robina?'

'No, Mama, they are not,' she responded, scrupulously honest, but with a hint of wistfulness which Lady Elizabeth's sharp ears had little difficulty in detecting.

She turned away from the window to look directly at her daughter once more. 'But you wish they were, is that it? You wish that during your time here in London you'd met just one young man who had succeeded in sending your heart pounding...? A knight in shining armour who might have swept you off your feet?' The sudden shout of laughter, though unexpected, lacked neither warmth nor sympathy. 'Ah, child, I was your age once and know what foolish fancies pass through a young girl's mind. Remember, my dear, that very few members of our class marry for love. And perhaps that is no bad thing... Love, after all, is a luxury few can afford.'

After a moment she moved slowly across to the door. 'Your father and I would never dream of forcing you into a marriage with a man you could neither like nor respect. I do not believe for a moment that you are indifferent to Lord Exmouth, child. So I would ask you to think long and hard before you turn down what might well prove to be your one and only chance of making a truly splendid match.'

Robina, watching the door being closed quietly, realised that her mother had divulged far more about herself during the past few minutes than ever before.

She had long held the belief that her parents' union had been a love-match. Lady Elizabeth Finedon, proud and aristocratic, the daughter of a duke, no less, had chosen to marry the Reverend William Perceval, a younger son of an impoverished baronet. If love had not been the reason for the union then Robina was at a loss to understand what it might have been. Maybe, though, during the passage of time, there had been occasions when her mother had regretted allowing her heart to rule her head.

Her father, a worthy man of rigid principles, had made no secret of the fact that it had been his wife's substantial dowry which had enabled him and his family to live in relative comfort, if not precisely luxury. Even so, it had been only the practising of strict economies over the years that had enabled the Vicar of Abbot Quincey and his wife to fund a London Season for their eldest daughter.

Robina knew that her parents had every intention of offering her three younger sisters the same opportunity as she herself had received. The twins,

Edwina and Frederica, would have their come-out next year, an even greater expense with two of them to launch. Little wonder, then, that her mother was wishful to see her eldest daughter suitably established before next spring.

Her conscience began to prick her as she gazed at the half-filled trunk. Her parents had found it no easy task to finance this enjoyable London Season. Her mother especially had deprived herself of so much over the years to ensure that each of her children possessed at least a small dowry to offer a prospective husband. Was it not time for the eldest daughter to show her appreciation by doing something in return?

She reached for the lovely gown which she had allowed to slip through her fingers a short time before and, folding it with care, placed it neatly on top of the other garments in the trunk.

Those perfectly matched greys which had momentarily captured Miss Robina Perceval's attention were brought to a halt some twenty minutes later outside a fashionable dwelling in Curzon Street. The middle-aged groom, sitting beside his master on the seat, willingly took charge of what he considered to be one of the finest pair of horses he'd seen in many a long year, and watched with a hint of pride as the greys' highly discerning owner jumped nimbly to the ground.

Although perhaps no longer in his first flush of youth, his master was none the less in the same prime physical condition as the animals he had purchased that very morning. Tall, lean and well-muscled, Lord Exmouth was still a fine figure of a man who, most people considered, was at last beginning to show definite signs of recovering from the tragic blow life had dealt him.

But there were those who knew better. There were those who knew the truth of it all and whose respect and devotion continued to hold them mute, Kendall mused, watching his master disappear inside the house.

Another prominent member of this touching band of loyal retainers was in the hall, ready to relieve his lordship of his hat and gloves. 'Her ladyship's compliments, my lord, and could you possibly spare her a few minutes of your time before incarcerating yourself away in your library.' The butler permitted himself a thin smile. 'Her ladyship's words, sir, not mine.'

'Where is the Dowager? Not still abed, I trust?'

'No, my lord. But still in her bedchamber, supervising the—er—packing of her trunks, I believe.'

White, even teeth flashed in a sportive smile. 'I

didn't suppose for a moment, Stebbings, that she was undertaking the task herself,' his lordship responded and, swiftly mounting the stairs, did not notice the butler's slightly stooping shoulders shaking in appreciative laughter.

Her ladyship, now well into middle age, was not renowned for exerting herself unduly, not if she could possibly avoid it. So it came as no great surprise to her lean, athletic son to discover her prostrate on the *chaise longue*, one podgy, be-ringed hand poised over the open box of sweetmeats too conveniently positioned nearby.

She paused before reducing the box's contents further to turn her head to see who had entered her room. 'Daniel, darling!' She greeted him with every evidence of delight, proffering one soft pink cheek upon which he might place a chaste salute, and then waiting for him to oblige her. 'I was informed you went out bright and early this morning. I sincerely trust you didn't forgo breakfast.'

'No, ma'am. You will be pleased to learn my appetite remains hale and hearty.'

'Yes, you do take after your dear papa in that, as in so many other things. He was not one to pick at his food, and yet he never seemed to put on an ounce of superfluous fat.' Her sigh was distinctly mournful. 'And yet here am I, eat like a bird, and have a girth like a Shetland pony!'

'Mmm, I wonder why?' his lordship murmured, casting a brief glance at the half-empty box at her elbow, before lowering his tall, lean frame, the envy of many of his friends, and much admired by more than one discerning female, into the chair nearby.

'You wished to see me, Mama?' he reminded her.

'Did I?' She looked decidedly vague, but as her son knew very well the Dowager's appearance was deceptive. She might have grown quite indolent in recent years, rarely bestirring herself if she could possibly avoid it, but little escaped the notice of those dreamy brown eyes. 'Ah, yes! It was only to remind you that the trunks are being sent on ahead today. We don't wish to be burdened with piles and piles of luggage when we set forth on Friday.'

'I believe Penn has seen to everything in his usual efficient way.'

'What a treasure that valet of yours is, Daniel! Just like my own dear Pinner.' She turned to the birdlike female, busily occupied in folding clothes into a sizeable trunk, and gave the faintest nod of dismissal.

'I trust you are looking forward to the forthcoming sojourn in Brighton, dear?' she continued the instant they were alone. 'And quite content to bear your feeble old mama company for several more weeks? I must confess I have thoroughly enjoyed our time together here in London.'

His lordship's eyes, so very like his mother's in both colour and shape, held a distinctly sardonic gleam. 'You are neither feeble-minded nor old, my dear. And neither am I a moonling. So you can stop trying to hoodwink me, and voice the question which is quivering on the tip of that occasionally ungovernable tongue of yours! Which is, of course, am I looking forward to furthering my acquaintance with Miss Perceval. The answer to which is…yes.'

His mother's gurgle of appreciative laughter was infectious, and his lordship found it impossible not to smile. 'Possibly just as well that I am anticipating a pleasant time by the sea, since Montague Merrell, together with half my acquaintance, is firmly convinced that the Reverend's delightful daughter would make me an ideal wife.'

'And so she would!' her ladyship agreed, not reluctant to add her voice to those which in recent weeks had urged the personable Baron to consider seriously taking the matrimonial plunge once again. 'She is without doubt the sweetest-natured gel you could ever wish to meet.'

'I wouldn't argue with that,' he agreed amicably. 'She is compliant and dutiful. She would never interfere with your pleasures, or cause you the least concern.'

'I should wish to know her a little better before voicing an opinion on certain aspects of her character.' He took a moment to study the nails on his left hand. 'I strongly suspect that Miss Robina Perceval possesses rather more spirit than most people realise.'

Her ladyship was inclined to take this as a criticism, but was not one hundred per cent sure that it was. Her son was one of those irritating people who always managed to conceal what they were thinking and feeling remarkably well. A disturbing possibility, and one which had never occurred to her before, did suddenly pass through her mind, however. 'I hope, my dear,' she said gently, 'that you were not hoping to find a second Clarissa. You never would, you know.'

His lordship regarded her in silence for a moment, his expression inscrutable, then he swiftly rose to his feet and went across to stand before the window, his body straight, but not noticeably tense.

'I realise that,' he said at length, his voice level and, like his expression, giving absolutely nothing away. 'Clarissa was undoubtedly a rare creature. I have yet to meet her equal in beauty… And I doubt I ever shall.'

Her ladyship, masterfully suppressing the threat of tears, looked across the room at him, at a loss to know quite how to respond. Not once since the tragedy occurred had he attempted to talk about the accident, at least not to her, and on the few occasions Clarissa's name had been mentioned she had watched him withdraw within himself, shrouding himself in his own private gloom.

'Do not look so stricken, my dear,' he advised gently, turning in time to catch that unmistakable expression, that look he had seen flit over scores of faces during these past months. 'I didn't come to London with the intention of searching for a mirror image of my dead wife. I came for the sole purpose of finding someone who would happily take care of my daughters, be kind to them and yes, I suppose, take the place of their dead mama.'

If this admission was supposed to relieve the Dowager's mind, it fell far short of the mark. 'I had hoped, Daniel, that you might have taken account of your own feelings in the matter, and not just your daughters' needs. Do you feel nothing for Miss Perceval at all?'

He was silent for so long that she thought he would refuse to satisfy her curiosity, but then he said, 'I think Robina Perceval is one of the most charming, good-natured and innately honest people I have ever met. I would feel a great deal easier in my mind, however, if I thought she really did wish to spend the summer with us in Brighton?'

'Daniel, whatever do you mean?'

She looked so utterly bewildered that it was as much as he could do not to laugh outright. 'Mama, I have always had the utmost respect for your acute understanding, but I must confess there have been occasions when you have allowed preconceived notions to cloud your judgement.'

'But—but…' The Dowager was momentarily lost for words. 'I'm sure you are wrong, Daniel. The dear child simply jumped at the opportunity to bear me company when I first asked her.'

'I do not doubt for a moment that she did, ma'am,' he concurred. 'It took me a short time only to discover that, although Miss Perceval possesses an innately charming reserve, she is by no means averse to socialising and has attained a great deal of pleasure during her time in London. Therefore it is quite natural that she would wish to continue the period of frivolous enjoyment if the opportunity arose. What appears to have escaped you completely, however, is the slight constraint in her which has been quite apparent to me since her return from Hampshire.'

The Dowager had not observed this. Which was extremely remiss of her, she decided, for she didn't doubt for a moment that her son, discerning demon that he was, had spoken no less than the truth. 'I wonder what could have occurred to make her have second thoughts about accompanying us?'

The look he cast her was more than faintly sardonic. 'Come, come, ma'am, isn't it obvious? Something or someone has made her realise what your real motive was for asking her in the first place.'

'How thoughtless some people are! And just when things were progressing so nicely too!' She looked as annoyed as it was possible for someone with her naturally amicable disposition to appear. 'Why must people interfere, Daniel?'

'Strangely enough, Mama, I have been asking myself that selfsame question during these past weeks,' he murmured, casting her a smile which managed to convey both loving affection and exasperation in equal measures. 'The damage has been done, however. She now knows what fate both you and her own mother have in store for her.'

'Daniel, that simply is not true!' She managed to hold his openly sardonic gaze for all of ten seconds before she made a great play of rearranging her shawl. 'I admit I may possibly have mentioned in passing that, now your official period of mourning had come to an end, you might be considering a second marriage.'

He raised his eyes heavenwards. 'You do surprise me!'

'And Lady Elizabeth may possibly have remarked on the fact that her eldest daughter, clearly betraying all the signs of truly motherly instincts, was unfailingly patient with her younger sisters,' she continued, just as though he had not spoken. 'But I assure you, Daniel, that I never suggested for a moment that I thought she would make an ideal wife for you. I would never dream of doing such a thing! You are far too much like your dear father. You are always willing to listen to someone else's viewpoint, but will make your own decision in the end.'

'I'm pleased you appreciate that at last, Mama, because it makes what I have to say to you now a great deal easier.' Although he was still faintly smiling, there was no mistaking the note of hard determination edging his deep, attractive voice. 'I was quite willing for you to cajole me into accompanying you to Brighton, even though I knew from the first your real motive for doing so... No, kindly allow me to finish,' he continued, holding up a restraining hand when she was about to interrupt. 'I wish to further my acquaintance with Miss Perceval, as I've already mentioned. She intrigues me. I believe there is much more to that young lady than either you or I realise. One thing I'm firmly convinced of, however, is that she had no thought of becoming the future Lady Exmouth until some well-meaning individual pointed out to her that that might well be the fate which awaits her. She may yet come to welcome that eventuality with open arms, but I am resolved that it shall be her decision, and not yours or her mother's... Now, do I make myself clear, my dear?'

'Perfectly, Daniel. You wish me to sit back, and allow nature to take its course.'

'Precisely!' The Dowager once again turned her attention to the tempting delicacies in the pretty box at her elbow. 'Very well, Daniel. You may woo Miss Robina Perceval in your own way, and without any interference from me.'

Narrow-eyed, Daniel watched a gooey confection disappear between smugly smiling pink lips. For some obscure reason he was not totally convinced that she would be able to keep that promise.

Chapter Two

Leaning back against the comfort of the velvet squabs, Lady Exmouth stared through the carriage window at the passing countryside, recalling quite clearly a time in the not too distant past when the road to Brighton had been little more than an uncertain track, frequently impassable. All that had changed, of course, once the Regent had discovered that the air at the small, insignificant resort tended to benefit his health. Now Brighton was a centre of fashion, and could be reached by many different routes, one of which was considered by many to be the finest posting road in England.

Her ladyship had happily left all the travel arrangements, and choice of route, in the hands of her very capable son. Since the age of one-and-twenty, when he had come into the title, Daniel had displayed a natural aptitude for organisation, and a keen sense of responsibility far beyond his years. Little wonder, the Dowager reflected, that only a very small number of people had voiced certain doubts when, just two years after his father's demise, he had calmly announced his intention of marrying his childhood sweetheart.

What a beautiful creature dear Clarissa had been! her ladyship mused, her mind's eye having little difficulty in conjuring up a clear image of limpid blue eyes set to perfection in that lovely heart-shaped face, the whole framed in a riot of the prettiest guinea-gold curls.

The only child of an impoverished country squire, Clarissa would undoubtedly have become the toast of any Season had her father ever been in a position to finance such a venture. From the age of sixteen she had had most every eligible young bachelor in the county dangling after her at one time or another. Yet she had remained touchingly devoted to the only son of her nearest neighbours. They had seemed such an ideal couple, perfectly suited in every way. When little Hannah had been born, within a year of their marriage, their happiness had seemed complete.

It had been shortly after the birth of her first grandchild, the Dowager clearly recalled, that she had first broached the subject of her making her home in Bath. It was most touching, of course, that neither her son nor daughter-in-law would hear of such a thing, so she had remained at Courtney Place until after the birth of their second child three years later. Then no amount of entreaties had persuaded her to remain in the beautiful ancestral home, where in many ways she had continued to feel as though she was still its mistress.

She had never experienced any regrets in the choice she had made. Bath suited her very well. She had made many friends there, and was looking forward to the day when she could return to her comfortable house in Camden Place.

Much depended, of course, on how matters progressed during these next few weeks in Brighton, for she had no intention of allowing her son to return to the ancestral pile alone, once the summer was over, to continue brooding over the loss of his lovely Clarissa. If this meant that she must delay her return to the West Country to bear him company, then so be it! She could not help hoping, though, that matters would resolve themselves in a far more satisfactory manner, and that her son would soon be sharing his lovely home with quite a different lady.

Drawing her eyes away from the pleasing landscape, her ladyship darted a glance at the only other occupant of the well-sprung travelling carriage to discover her companion sitting quietly staring out of the other window, seemingly lost in a world of her own.

Daniel, the astute demon, had not been wrong when he had suggested that something had occurred to disturb the normally very calm waters of Miss Robina Perceval's mind. Something most definitely had! If, as Daniel himself suspected, the vicar's daughter was not at all sure that she wished to cement an alliance with the noble Courtney family, then it would, indeed, be most unfair to bring pressure to bear upon the dear girl during the forthcoming weeks to do just that.

It was so difficult to know how best to proceed in a situation such as this, her ladyship decided, absently running a finger back and forth across a faint crease in her skirts. She had no real desire to interfere in such a delicate and personal matter, while at the same time she had no intention of allowing her only child to dwindle into middle age a lonely and grieving man, when at hand was the very being who could bring great contentment back into his life, even if she failed to make him perfectly happy.

It wasn't as if she was foolish enough to suppose for a moment that Miss Robina Perceval could ever take the place of the beautiful Clarissa in Daniel's eyes. That would be hoping for far too much! There was no denying, though, that he had perceived something in the vicar's daughter that appealed to him, for she was the only female he had displayed the least interest in throughout his entire sojourn in the capital.

She cast a further glance across the carriage to the opposite corner. Only this time she discovered that she was being observed in turn by a pair of blue eyes which, although of a similar hue, betrayed a deal more intelligence than the late Baroness Exmouth's had ever done.

'I was beginning to think you'd fallen asleep,' her ladyship remarked for want of something better to say. 'So quiet had you become.'

'Oh, no, my lady. Merely lost in admiration for this part of the country. I've never travelled this far south before, so everything is new and interesting.'

Although the poor girl might be experiencing grave doubts about this forthcoming sojourn in Brighton, it was quite evident that she was not prepared to brood about it to the extent that she became taciturn, the Dowager thought, mentally adding a further tick to that long column of Miss Robina Perceval's excellent qualities.

'I can recall a time, my dear child, not so very long ago, when many abandoned their attempts to reach the small fishing village, which Brighton used to be not so very long ago. Much is said these days to the Regent's discredit, but if he had not purchased his "little farmhouse" on the coast, I very much fear that this and many other roads in this part of the country would have remained those frequently impassable tracks, full of potholes and littered with abandoned carriages.'

Evidently the vicar's eldest daughter was much struck by this viewpoint, for her pretty face wore a very thoughtful expression, as it so often did when she was turning something over in her mind.

'Yes, one tends to forget that not so very long ago travelling about the country was something of a dangerous undertaking, and that journeys that used to take very many hours are now completed in a fraction of the time.'

'And in far greater comfort, too!' her ladyship assured her. 'Carriages are so well sprung nowadays, and there are always plenty of hostelries *en route* where one can refresh oneself.'

As if on cue the carriage turned off the post road a moment later and came to a halt in the forecourt of a very superior posting-house. The door was thrown wide, the steps were let down, and his lordship stood, hand held out, ready and appearing very willing, to assist them to alight.

'Why is it, Mama,' he remarked, guiding them into the inn, 'that two ladies can travel the same distance, in the very same conveyance, and yet one can look none the worse for her ordeal whilst the other resembles nothing so much as a ruffled hen which has spent much of the day ineffectually flapping about a farmyard?'

'Odious boy! No need to enquire which of us in your opinion needs to set her appearance to rights, I suppose.' The Dowager tried to appear affronted but failed miserably. 'Where may this overheated hen refresh herself?'

His lordship beckoned to a serving-maid, and Robina, having somehow managed to keep her countenance, accompanied her ladyship into one of the upstairs chambers to effect the necessary repairs to her own appearance.

It was by no means the first time she had heard Daniel utter some provocative remark. Her ladyship never failed to take her son's teasing in good part, and Robina couldn't help but feel a little envious of the special bond which existed between mother and son. She would never have dreamt of saying such things to either of her parents, especially not to her mother, who, unlike the Dowager, did not possess much of a sense of humour.

That was perhaps why she liked her ladyship so much. Lady Exmouth was such an easygoing soul, fun-loving yet in no way light-minded, though she tried, Robina had frequently suspected, to give the impression that she was a trifle featherbrained.

They had got on famously from the first, and Robina did not doubt that she would have derived much pleasure from the Dowager's delightful company during the forthcoming weeks, had it not been for the fact that that dear lady would be bitterly disappointed if, by the end of their stay in Brighton, her son's engagement to the Vicar of Abbot Quincey's daughter had not been announced.

She ought to feel flattered, she supposed, that the Dowager's son had taken such an interest in her, and maybe she would have been if she thought for a moment that she had succeeded in capturing his heart. But she flatly refused to delude herself. There was little hope of her, or anyone else for that matter, ever taking the place of his late wife.

After removing her bonnet, she took a moment to study her reflection in the glass as she tidied an errant curl. She was well enough, she supposed.

At least she had been assured that she was pretty enough to turn heads, but that did not make her a beauty. Yet, there had been beauties enough gracing the Season that year, she reminded herself, her friend Sophia Cleeve to name but one. So wasn't it rather odd that Lord Exmouth had displayed precious little interest in any one of them if he was indeed the connoisseur of beauty he was reputed to be?

'Something appears to be troubling you, child?'

Jolted out of her puzzling reflections, Robina discovered that she was the focal point of a deceptively dreamy brown-eyed gaze. 'Er—no, not really, my lady. I was just thinking of certain persons I had seen during the recent Season in London, and was wondering how many would be following our example by removing to Brighton.'

Robina salved her conscience by telling herself that it was not a complete lie, and fortunately the Dowager seemed to accept the explanation readily enough.

'A great many, I shouldn't wonder. Certainly the Carlton House set, one of whom, as you probably know, is none other than my son's particular friend, Montague Merrell. We'll ask Daniel who is likely to be paying a visit to the town, should we? No doubt he'll enlighten us.'

This, however, he seemed unable, or disinclined, to do, when they joined him a few minutes later in a private parlour. He merely shrugged, saying, 'You know I'm not one of the Regent's cronies, Mama. And I cannot say that I'm in the least interested in who'll be trailing after him this summer.'

'For a young man who has been considered one of the *ton's* most fashionable members all his adult life, you display precious little interest in what goes on in polite society,' his mother remarked, casting an approving glance over the delicious fare awaiting her on the table.

Daniel was not slow to observe the rapacious gleam in those dark eyes, and obliged her by pulling out one of the chairs. As far as he could recall his mother had always been blessed with a healthy appetite. Which was no very bad thing, he didn't suppose, so long as one did not permit food to become a ruling passion.

He had not been slow to note, either, that Miss Perceval had not opened that immensely kissable mouth of hers since entering the room; had noticed too that she appeared increasingly ill-at-ease in his company these days. A decidedly sorry state of affairs which must be rectified without delay!

'Permit me to help you to a slice or two of

chicken, Miss Perceval.' He did so without offering her the opportunity to refuse. 'You must be hungry after spending so many hours in a carriage. Travelling any great distance often makes one feel peckish.'

'It certainly has that effect on me,' the Dowager put in.

'That goes without saying, Mama.'

'Rude boy!' she admonished good-humouredly. 'Your dear papa did not beat you enough when you were a child.'

Daniel noticed that sweet, spontaneous smile, hurriedly suppressed, at the foolish banter, and was fairly sure that it would be no hard matter to restore the delectable Robina to her former composed state. Perhaps it might even be possible to achieve a closer bond between them before the day was out, he decided, swiftly setting himself a new goal.

'I dare say you are right, Mama. However, permit me to point out that there is a delicious game pie lurking by your right elbow which appears to have escaped your notice.'

'Thank you, my dear.' A flicker of a knowing smile hovered around her ladyship's mouth, clearly betraying to her son that she knew precisely what he was about. It appeared to be having the required effect too, for their guest began to help herself to the various tempting dishes on offer without the least prompting.

'I must say, my dear boy, you have surpassed yourself. This is a most marvellous repast you have ordered, catering for all tastes.'

'Nothing whatever to do with me,' he surprised them both by admitting. 'If you wish to express your appreciation, then thank Kendall. He was the one who bespoke this late luncheon to be served in a private parlour when he arranged for the stabling of my greys here two days ago.'

'Have we very much farther to travel, my lord?' Robina enquired, deciding that it was high time she added something to the conversation.

'There's about an hour's journey ahead of us, certainly no more. My latest acquisitions will accomplish it easily.'

'You are delighted with your greys, are you not, my son?'

'Exceedingly, ma'am!' he concurred, looking extremely pleased with himself. 'It was very gratifying to pip no less a personage than a duke to the post in purchasing them. I was reliably informed that Sharnbrook was more than a little interested,' he informed them in response to their enquiring glances, 'but he delayed too long. Possibly had more important things on his mind, like his engagement to Miss Perceval's friend, for instance.'

'Now that rather insignificant affair surprised me,' her ladyship remarked. 'I do not understand at all why they held such a small party at Sharnbrook to celebrate the event. After all, the Duke is reputed to be one of the richest men in England. It's not as if he couldn't afford a large affair. Your friend's papa too, Robina, is held to be very plump in the pocket, so I fail to understand why the engagement wasn't celebrated more lavishly.'

'It was what Sophia and Benedict both wanted,' Robina divulged. 'I know it was only a small party, but it was a most enjoyable occasion none the less.'

'I'm all in favour of keeping these highly personal celebrations as small and informal as possible,' his lordship announced, surprising his mother somewhat. 'I could almost feel guilty now at depriving Sharnbrook of those superb greys. I should imagine we have much in common. Just because one happens to be comfortably circumstanced does not mean that one needs to make a vulgar display of the fact.'

'You do surprise me, my son. You insisted that

half the county be invited to the party celebrating your engagement to Clarissa.'

The Dowager had spoken without thinking, and cursed herself silently for every kind of a fool. She had rarely mentioned her late daughter-in-law's name when in public, and never in front of the young woman who now sat silently at the table and who appeared totally absorbed in devouring the food on her plate.

'Very true, Mama,' his lordship responded, swiftly breaking the ensuing silence, and betraying no visible signs of distress at touching on such a poignant subject. 'But a person's taste can change over the years. 'I would at one time never have considered driving myself above a few miles in an open carriage, but have very much enjoyed the experiences of this day.'

His dark eyes flickered momentarily in Robina's direction. 'Perhaps I can persuade you, Miss Perceval, to bear me company for what remains of the journey. You might find travelling in the fresh air a more pleasurable way of completing the journey. Added to which, it will permit her ladyship to close her eyes, as is her custom in the afternoons, without appearing rude.'

Robina hesitated, but only for a moment. There was no earthly way that she was going to be able to avoid his lordship's company for any appreciable lengths of time during the forthcoming weeks, so she might as well be sensible and accustom herself to his presence at the outset.

'Yes, my lord, I think a spell in the fresh air would be most welcome.' She cast him a smile which somehow managed to display both a hint of shyness and a touch of roguery. 'I might end looking slightly windswept, but at least I hope I shall avoid resembling some demented hen.'

His deep rumble of appreciative laughter succeeded in putting her at her ease to such an extent that when, a short while later, she was seated beside him in the curricle, she was more than content to be in his company, and not in the least nervous over placing her well-being in the hands of a man who had, reputedly through the dangerous tooling of a carriage, succeeded in killing his beloved wife.

It was only, after happily following the comfortable vehicle containing his mother for a mile or so, when his lordship unexpectedly turned off the main post road and on to a much narrower lane, bringing the spirited greys to a halt beneath the shade of some roadside trees, that she began to experience those stabs of blind panic which had plagued her from time to time during recent days.

'Miss Perceval, I had a particular reason for wishing you to bear me company for the remainder of the journey,' he announced, staring straight ahead down the deserted road, while with little effort, it seemed, masterfully controlling his spirited horses. 'If my mother performs her duties as your chaperon conscientiously, there ought not to be too many occasions when we find ourselves quite alone together, and there is something I particularly wished to say to you before we embark on what I hope will be a most enjoyable stay for us both in Brighton.'

If Robina had not felt as if she were being slowly throttled she would quite happily have betrayed her feelings by giving vent to a loud and protracted groan. She had forced herself to come to terms with the fact that sooner or later the subject of a marriage between them would be raised, but she had hoped that the occasion would arise later rather than sooner, thereby permitting her to enjoy a brief period in Brighton without encumbrance. His lordship began speaking again, and she forced herself to listen.

'We both know why our respective mothers wished us to spend the summer together. They are both hoping that I shall—to resort to the modern-day vulgar parlance—come up to scratch. Well, let me assure you, Miss Perceval, that at this present moment in time I have not the slightest intention of making you an offer of marriage.'

Turning his head, Daniel discovered a look of such utter bewilderment on her sweet face that he was forced to exert every ounce of control he possessed not to take her into his arms and totally confound her by kissing her breathless.

'You look slightly stunned, Miss Perceval.' An understatement if ever there was one. The poor girl looked as if she were about to swoon! 'I'm sorry if my plain speaking has offended you.'

'Er—no, not at all, sir,' she responded so softly that he had a little difficulty in catching the words.

'But I think we would rub along much more comfortably if we cleared up one or two matters at the outset.' Again he was forced to exert the utmost control, only this time to stop himself from laughing. She was regarding him much as defenceless rabbit might a snake which was about to strike for a second time. 'I think you must realise, Miss Perceval, that I have grown quite partial to your company during our time in London. I should like to think that we have become…friends.'

'Er—yes,' she responded guardedly.

'And as such, I think we can be honest with each other without causing offence.'

'It—er—would be nice to think we could, certainly,' she agreed, in a voice that was growing progressively stronger, though remaining slightly wary at the same time.

'As you may have gathered by now, my darling mother, together with most of my friends, has decided that it is high time I consider a second marriage.'

No response was forthcoming this time, so he continued undeterred. 'It seems that most are in agreement that you would make me the ideal wife.'

Again there was no response.

'They may possibly be correct, but I reserve the right to decide for myself. Just as I believe that you deserve the chance to make up your mind about me, without the least pressure being brought to bear upon you. That could be difficult in the present circumstances, with a certain person watching our every move, waiting with bated breath for us to announce our betrothal, unless we both work together to turn the situation in which we now find ourselves to our mutual advantage.'

She appeared merely bewildered now as she said, 'And how do you propose that we do that, my lord?'

'Simply by just being ourselves, and doing precisely what we wish to do. It would be foolish to attempt to avoid one another, as we'll be residing in the same house, don't you agree?'

'Most assuredly.'

'So what I suggest is that we keep the world guessing by being seen in each other's company quite frequently, while at the same time not denying ourselves the pleasure of other people's.' He continued to hold her full attention. 'Then, if by the end of the summer, when we have come to know each other a good deal better, we both decide that we should suit, all well and good, and if not...'

He reached for one of her hands and felt those slender, tapering fingers momentarily tremble in his clasp. 'Either way, child, I want the decision to be ours, yours and mine. Not your mother's, or mine, or anyone else's, understand?'

It took a monumental effort, but Robina forced herself to meet his concerned and kindly gaze, and made a rather startling discovery. His eyes were not just a deep, warm brown but were flecked rather attractively with gold.

'Yes, my lord, I do understand... And—and thank you,' she said softly, blissfully ignorant of the fact that it had cost him dearly to suggest what he had, that the last thing in the world he had wanted was to release her from any obligations she might feel to marry him.

'For what, silly child?' His expressive brows rose. 'For suggesting something that will benefit us both? Well, if you wish to show your appreciation, you can kindly stop calling me my lord. My name is Daniel.'

'Oh, I couldn't possibly address you like that, sir!' She was genuinely shocked. 'Mama would never approve.'

'I'm not particularly interested whether she would or not,' he returned bluntly. 'You'll be residing under my roof for the next few weeks, my girl, so you'll do what I tell you, especially if you know what's good for you.'

She gave an uncertain laugh. By repute he was a kind-hearted, considerate man, and yet some inner feminine wisdom warned her that there might be a less agreeable side to him if he was ever crossed. She had already discovered that he was not afraid to speak his mind, and couldn't help wondering what other interesting facets to his character would emerge before this day was out.

'Very well, little bird, we'll compromise. When in private I insist you call me Daniel, and when in public you may call me what ever you like...'

white teeth flashed in a playful smile '...providing it is polite, of course.'

Giving the little hand a last reassuring squeeze, Daniel turned his attention back to the greys. 'We had better catch up with my darling mama, otherwise she might imagine we've eloped.'

'Oh, how excessively romantic!' Robina exclaimed without thinking, and then turned a glowing crimson when she discovered herself on the receiving end of a startled glance.

'Excessively uncomfortable, I would have thought,' he contradicted, slowing his team down as they approached a busy little village, 'especially if undertaken in an equipage such as this one, and it should come on to rain.'

'People in love would not consider such a mundane thing as the weather, if they were considering running away together,' she pointed out, rather enjoying his teasing banter, and liking too the way his eyes were brightened by that wickedly provocative glint.

'I should,' he argued, 'but then I'm a practical sort of person, not given to mad starts. Besides which, having attained the great age of almost six-and-thirty, I enjoy my creature comforts and am far too old to go careering about the country. So I can tell you now, I shall never consider eloping with you.'

'In that case, I think you were very wise to have second thoughts about making me an offer,' she informed him quite deliberately, knowing that even half an hour ago she would never have considered saying such a thing to him. Now, however, she felt as if a very close friendship was on the verge of springing up between them. 'It is quite evident to me at least that we would not have suited. I should very much like a gentleman to go careering about the country with me.'

'I never said that I had had second thoughts about making you an offer, my girl,' he corrected. 'I merely said— What the devil!'

For a moment Robina was startled, then she saw it too—a great brute of a man beating a donkey with a stout stick, and very much appearing as if he was enjoying the exercise, while a woman, with two children frantically clutching at the folds of her skirts, was alternately shouting and pleading with him to stop.

Without a second thought Robina accepted the reins Daniel tossed into her hands, and then watched him stalk across the road. Easily capturing the stick, he proceeded to lay it about the bully's shoulders before calmly knocking him to the ground with one superbly aimed blow to the jaw.

She was a little too far away to hear clearly what was being said, but a great deal of gesticulating, and swearing, she suspected, especially on the part of the felled bully, followed as Daniel calmly took something from inside his right boot. A moment later the pile of pots and pans which had been tied to the donkey's back fell to the ground with a clatter, and a further heated altercation between the man and the woman ensued, before Daniel stepped into the breach once again.

Robina was only vaguely aware of what followed, for her attention was taken up with calming the greys, which had taken exception to the noise of the pots and pans clattering on the road. By the time she had them well under control again, the unkempt rogue was trudging off up the village street, carrying his wares on his own back, the two children, no longer sobbing, were leading the donkey into a paddock, and Daniel was accompanying the woman into a charming thatched cottage.

He reappeared a few minutes later, the woman at his heels this time, desperately striving to keep up with his long-striding gait, while attempting to offer her grateful thanks.

'Not at all, my good woman. Only too pleased

to be of assistance,' Robina heard him say, before he doffed his hat, and came hurriedly across the road towards her.

'My dear girl, I cannot apologise enough!' There was an unmistakable flicker of concern in his eyes as he clambered up on the seat and relieved her of the reins. 'What on earth must you think of me, deserting you in such a fashion! I sincerely trust you weren't too nervous at being left in charge of the greys?'

'Not at all,' she assured him. 'I frequently tool Papa's one-horse gig when at home.' She caught the slight twitch at the corner of his mouth, but didn't attempt to enquire precisely what he had found so amusing, and merely asked for an account of what had taken place.

'You saw what happened, I am ashamed to say, but there was little I could do to avoid your witnessing that unfortunate encounter.' He gave the greys the office to start, once again handling the spirited pair with effortless ease. 'I am not accounted a violent man, and yet I would be the first to admit that I have an almost pathological hatred for persons who inflict needless cruelty. It wasn't sufficient for that oaf to pass by the gate of the donkey's former, caring owners each day, he must needs stop to torment those children further by abusing a creature they both love, and had looked upon as a pet.'

'How dreadful! I'm very glad we happened along. And now the donkey, I assume, has been restored to its former owners.'

'Not quite.' His smile was decidedly rueful. 'He now belongs to me. I decided, all things considered, that it would be for the best.'

Robina managed to keep her countenance, but it was an effort. It was quite evident that he wasn't precisely enthusiastic over this latest acquisition, and she could not resist the temptation to tease him a little.

'I have observed during my weeks in London that it is not unusual for a gentleman of—how shall I phrase it?—an eccentric nature to indulge in rather queer starts from time to time. I suppose you suddenly discovered that you had need of a beast of burden?'

'I am beginning to discover that there is a strong teasing element in your nature, my girl!' The swift, narrow-eyed glance he cast her managed to betray both amusement and faint exasperation. 'No, you provoking little baggage! I did not suddenly take it into my head that I wished to own such a creature. And if you dare to tell another living soul, you'll regret it! I would become a laughingstock, and the talk of the clubs for weeks!'

She did not suppose for a moment that he would care a jot what the world at large said or thought about him, but she gave her solemn promise none the less, before demanding to know why he had taken it upon himself to make such an odd purchase.

'Because I discovered that it was in fact that poor woman's idle husband who sold the beast, before calmly going off and leaving her and their children to fend for themselves. She hasn't seen him since and doesn't expect to. There is, however, always the chance that he'll turn up again, like the proverbial bad penny, and repeat the procedure, leaving her without the means to transport her goods to market, and depriving the children of their pet. So to overcome this possibility, I have given her a letter which states that, on condition she takes good care of the animal, she has my full permission, as its owner, to use the donkey to transport her goods to the local market, but on no account must my property be sold without my written consent.'

How exceedingly kind and considerate he was! Robina decided, as they rejoined the post road and she caught sight of her ladyship's carriage in the distance. He had been generous to three perfect strangers and no less generous towards her.

By demanding only friendship, he had now made it possible for her to enjoy the weeks ahead without fear that at the end of her stay she would be asked for recompense.

So why then, she wondered, a frown of puzzlement creasing her brow, wasn't she feeling deliriously happy at this precise moment? Furthermore, why had she suddenly developed this peculiar hollow feeling deep inside?

Chapter Three

Robina, still very much enjoying the novel experience of having her hair expertly dressed each day by Lady Exmouth's skilful abigail, sat quietly before the dressing-table mirror, contemplating yet again how much her life had changed since she had left rural Northamptonshire behind her on that cold day in early March.

For a simple country girl, accustomed to comfort rather than luxury, and to lengthy periods of solitude, given to quiet reflection, or the pursuit of some useful occupation whereby she might be of some benefit to her fellow man, it was quite surprising the ease with which she had conformed to a hectic and purely social life, where the pursuit of personal pleasure was the only thing that need concern her to any degree. Her mother's presence, understandably, had been a steadying influence during those heady weeks in London. Since her arrival in Brighton no restrictions had been placed upon her whatsoever. In fact, not to put too fine a point on it, she was being thoroughly spoilt by the darling Dowager and her no less considerate son. And she was shamefully loving every moment of it!

'It's simply no good at all. It must stop!' she announced, with as much determination as she could muster, and without really realising that she had spoken her guilty thoughts aloud until she happened to glance up and noticed the middle-aged abigail's slightly puzzled expression in the dressing-table mirror.

'What's the matter, miss? Don't you care for this style any longer? We can always try something different if you'd prefer.'

'I have no fault to find with the way you dress my hair, Pinner,' Robina hurriedly assured her.

'Well, that's a blessing, miss!' One could almost sense that the highly skilled and conscientious servant was suppressing a sigh of relief. 'For one dreadful moment there I thought you were going to ask me to cut it. And that I would never willingly do,' she announced, easing the brush almost reverently through the long shiny dark strands.

'Beautiful, it is, and a sheer delight to dress, miss, just like the rest of you. There aren't too many blessed with such a perfect figure as yours. You're an abigail's dream, Miss Robina, so you are! You'd look wonderfully turned out in a scullery-maid's apron!'

'You're the one who deserves the credit, not I,' Robina countered, desperately striving not to allow this fulsome praise go to her head.

As her father, the Reverend William Perceval, had always considered vanity amongst the very worst of sins, compliments were rarely uttered back at the vicarage in Abbot Quincey, and yet Robina, who had been taught to consider inner beauty far more meaningful than any shallow outward trappings, could not help but feel gratified by the compliment.

'It is no good, Pinner,' she announced, rising to her feet when the last curls had been carefully pinned into place. 'I must face the fact that, unless I begin to exert a deal of self-control, I stand in the gravest danger of becoming thoroughly corrupted whilst I continue to reside under this roof. Why, I shall be of no earthly use to man or beast when the time comes for me to return to Abbot Quincey! I never used to think twice about mending a tear in a gown, or dressing my own hair.

Now I wouldn't even contemplate doing such a thing, and am more than content to sit back and allow others to do everything for me. Thoroughly indulged, I am, and loving it! What would dear Papa say?'

It was all very well to make light of it, Robina decided, as the bedchamber resounded with Pinner's highly amused chuckles, but really it was no laughing matter. She had adapted to this life of ease, this life of pure self-indulgence, as though she had been born to it, which of course was far from the truth. Although life at the vicarage could never have been described as one of drudgery, she had been expected to undertake a variety of light duties, which had included a certain amount of time given to the entertainment of her three younger sisters, ensuring that they didn't get into mischief by setting a good example herself.

And a fine example she would set for them now! she mused, unable to suppress a rueful half-smile. There was no denying that the highly complaisant and faintly indolent Dowager was an appalling influence. To be fair, though, she ought to accept the lion's share of the blame herself for not displaying more strength of character and halting her meteoric descent into that wicked pit of dissipation. On the other hand, it had to be said in her own defence that she had been battling against tremendous odds during these past days. Why, even his lordship had actively encouraged her to do precisely as she wished!

Although Daniel had made his feelings on the matter perfectly clear at the outset by announcing that friendship was all he demanded from her at this present moment in time, since their arrival in Brighton he had been unfailingly thoughtful, touchingly attentive to her every possible need.

She paused as she reached the bottom of the stairs, and stared thoughtfully in the direction of the breakfast-parlour door, unaware that her expression had been softened by a quite spontaneous, tender little smile.

She found it hard to believe now, but it was true none the less that, although she had readily agreed to the suggestion when it had first been made, she had, surprisingly, not found it easy to look upon Daniel merely as a friend. Which was all the more curious because she had never found it in the least daunting to converse with him, not even when they had first met in London.

Her father's particular calling had ensured that throughout her life she had, on a fairly regular basis, come into contact with people who had suffered recent bereavement. Consequently she had known precisely what to say to Daniel from the first, and had never experienced the least awkwardness in his presence. A slightly closer relationship had initially, she was forced to own, proved a different matter entirely, however.

Not having been blessed with any brothers had, she supposed, substantially limited her experience of the opposite sex, and although her Perceval cousins, Hugo and Lowell, had been frequent visitors to the vicarage, she had acquired precious little knowledge of the workings of the male mind from either of them. During childhood she had been inclined to look upon Hugo, some ten years her senior, as a most superior being, sophisticated, charming, and slightly unapproachable; Lowell, being some six years his brother's junior, had always seemed to her, and still did for that matter, little more than an endearing scamp, always ripe for any lark. Consequently, living under the same roof as Lord Exmouth had turned out to be something of a revelation.

Daniel, she had swiftly discovered, possessed the most wonderful sense of humour. He certainly appeared to enjoy indulging in bouts of lighthearted banter, and the frequent exchange of the swift repartee, but there was nothing of the mischievous schoolboy in his nature. Far from it, in fact! He was every inch the fashionable gentleman, accomplished and refined, and yet not remotely high in the instep. This was perhaps why she had managed eventually to dispense with those last barriers of reserve, and had come to feel so completely relaxed in his company, more so, surprisingly, than in her own father's.

No one would have supposed for a moment that Robina held her new-found friend in such high esteem when she entered the breakfast-parlour a moment later to discover him, as expected, already seated at the table; least of all Daniel himself, who was not slow to perceive the slightly troubled look in her strikingly pretty, clear blue eyes.

'What's the matter, my little bird?' Ever the polite gentleman, he rose to his feet and waited until she had slipped into the chair beside his own before resuming his repast. 'Did you have trouble sleeping last night?'

'How could I possibly have trouble sleeping, Daniel, when I have been given, I do not doubt, the most comfortable bed in the house?' Without the least show of reticence, Robina began to help herself to coffee and a delicious hot buttered roll. 'And that is precisely what concerns me. If I'm not very careful, I'm likely to be ruined by both you and your mother.'

'Now there's a tempting thought!' he muttered before he could stop himself, but fortunately she appeared not to have heard. 'How precisely have Mama and I fallen from grace?'

'You both spoil me shamefully. Yes, you do,' she reiterated when he looked about to refute this. 'You have been so kind, giving up so much of your time in order to keep me entertained. And as for your mother… Oh, Daniel! She came to my bedchamber after we had retired last night, bringing the box containing that lovely garnet necklace of hers and matching earrings.' There was no mistaking the agitation in her voice. 'She insisted on making me a present of them, and I found myself in the position whereby to have refused would have made me appear so very ungrateful. And that I assure you I am not! But she really ought not to give me such things.'

'I couldn't agree more!' he announced, surprising her somewhat, for he sounded genuinely annoyed.

'Then—then, you'll have a word with her on—on my behalf?' she ventured, fervently hoping that she would not be causing trouble between mother and son. 'Suggesting kindly, I hope, that she ought not to—to give me such things?'

'Most assuredly I shall, child. You may rely

upon it,' he responded, frowning dourly as the door opened. 'And there's no time like the present,' he added as the object of his evident displeasure, joining them early for once, entered the breakfast-parlour.

'What's this I've been hearing, Mama!' he demanded the instant she had seated herself in the chair opposite. 'What do you mean by presenting Robin with that set of garnets, may I ask?'

'Why shouldn't I, dear?' the Dowager replied, betraying no obvious signs of resentment at the faintly dictatorial tone. 'They were mine to dispose of as I saw fit, and they will look much prettier displayed against young skin.' Glancing across the table, she was not slow to notice the twinkling mischief in his dark eyes. 'What is the matter, my son? Do you disapprove of my giving Robina such a gift?'

'Most assuredly! Why didn't you present her with the rubies?' Daniel almost burst out laughing as Robina's knife fell from her fingers to land on her plate with a clatter. 'I've always considered garnets trumpery gauds, as well you know.'

'Well, dear, I couldn't give her the ruby set, now could I?' the Dowager pointed out in her defence. 'They are amongst the family jewels, and are kept safely locked away at Courtney Place. Besides which, they are not mine to give.'

Ignoring the flashing look of reproach from a certain highly disgruntled quarter, Daniel leaned back in his chair, looking for all the world as if he were giving the matter due consideration. 'I do not think I would give Robin the ruby set in any case, not unless she had her heart set on them, that is. No, I would be more inclined, with her delicate colouring, to deck her out in sapphires. What do you think, Mama?'

'Oh, for heaven's sake!' Robina buried her face in her hands, not knowing whether to laugh or cry. 'I give up!'

'Yes, you may have a point there, dear,' her ladyship agreed, sublimely ignoring the muttered interruption. 'Sapphires certainly emphasise blue eyes and a fair complexion, but don't discount the rubies, my son. With that beautiful dark hair, she could carry that particular stone very well, too.'

Wickedly enjoying himself at his darling guest's expense, his lordship finished off the last mouthful on his plate before reaching for the journal conveniently placed nearby. 'By the by, Mama. Darling Robina, here, feels that we are spoiling her, and being far, far too kind. So I have decided to remedy this misconduct on our part by taking her out in the curricle this morning.'

A brief glance in Robina's direction was sufficient to inform the Dowager that the girl was as much puzzled by this pronouncement as she was herself. 'I'm evidently being foolishly obtuse, but I do not immediately perceive how jaunting about the town in an open carriage is likely to remedy the situation, my son.'

'Because yesterday, when Robin and I were strolling about the town, our attention was momentarily captured by the sight of that outrageous Lady Claudia Melrose making an exhibition of herself again by tooling a high-perched phaeton down the middle of the street. And young madam here, far from scandalised by such behaviour, was not slow to express her admiration of the dashing lady's skill, nor her wish that she too could tool a racing vehicle with such flair. So, after due consideration, I've decided to offer the benefit of my no little experience and instruct her.'

Robina, swiftly forgetting her grievances, gave vent to a tiny squeal of delight. 'Truly, sir...? You'll teach me?'

'Yes, child, but only because it will offer me the golden opportunity of scolding you unmercifully, you understand? And woe betide you if you dare to damage my greys' delicate—'

He broke off, staring fixedly for a few moments at the article in the newspaper which had unexpectedly captured his attention, before handing the journal over to Robina, indicating the section he wished her to read by prodding the precise spot in the column with one well-manicured finger. 'Am I right in thinking that the Marquis of Sywell heralded from your neck of the woods, child?'

Her expression changing to one of incredulity, Robina swiftly apprised herself of the item of news, and then automatically turned to Daniel for corroboration. 'Heavens above! Do you suppose it can possibly be true?'

'I am on occasions very sceptical about what I read in the newspapers, most especially about what appears in the gossip columns. But I doubt very much that such a detailed account as that one would have appeared in print if it were not true.'

'What on earth has happened?' the Dowager enquired, gaining her son's attention.

'The Marquis of Sywell is dead. He was discovered by his manservant lying flat on his back on the bedchamber floor, with a razor—er—stuck in his chest. It may have been an accident of course. Sywell was, after all, a notorious drunkard who could well have tripped and fallen on the implement. The authorities, however, cannot rule out foul play.'

'No, indeed,' Robina agreed, focusing her attention on an imaginary spot on the wall opposite, wondering why she felt not the smallest degree of remorse.

Undeniably, the Marquis had been a cruel, thoroughly selfish man who had gone through life taking what he wanted, when he wanted, with no consideration whatsoever for the feelings of others. The name Sywell had become a byword for debauchery among the inhabitants of the four Abbey villages. He had been despised by many; liked by none. He had not, however, inflicted any harm on her personally, nor on any member of her immediate family, as far as she was aware. So surely she ought to feel at least a twinge of remorse, if not for his death, then at least for the manner of his passing? The truth of the matter was, though, she felt absolutely nothing at all, and was not quite comfortable with herself for this sad absence of feeling. Had her weeks in London so changed her that she now cared not a whit whether or not a fellow human being had met his end in so violent a manner?

Daniel, watching her closely, was not slow to

note the slightly perturbed expression. 'Were you well acquainted with him, child?'

'No, not at all.' She shook her head in wonder. 'It is a shameful thing to admit to,' she announced, not thinking twice about sharing her thoughts with him, 'but I think the world will be a better place without the Marquis. If my sympathies rest with anyone, then it is with the possible perpetrator of the deed. What he must have suffered at Sywell's hands to induce him to seek revenge and commit such an act one can only wonder at.'

'Very true,' the Dowager agreed, much struck by this. 'And if he was indeed murdered, I doubt there will be any lack of suspects.'

'I didn't realise you were so well acquainted with him, Mama?'

'We were slightly acquainted, Daniel,' she corrected him. 'We met on one or two occasions many years ago. Your maternal grandfather was not in favour of a closer association. Even in those days Sywell had a somewhat unsavoury reputation. He was undeniably a most disagreeable man, who went through life making enemies—far more, I dare say, than there will be mourners at his funeral to lament his passing.'

'You may possibly be right,' Daniel agreed, rising to his feet. 'But I for one have no intention of fruitlessly trying to speculate on which of his numerous enemies might have been the perpetrator of the crime—if indeed a crime was committed, for that in itself has yet to be proved. I have a far more important matter taxing my poor brain at this present moment in time—namely, how to pacify Kendall for the ordeal ahead of him.

'You may or may not be aware of it, ma'am,' he continued, in response to the faintly bewildered glance his mother cast up at him as he passed her chair, 'but my most loyal retainer, being a confirmed bachelor, retains one or two preconceived notions where the fair sex is concerned. He is not a total misogynist, for he has on the odd occasion been overheard to utter mild praise when observing some female equestrian displaying a modicum of skill. He is, however, old-fashioned enough to deplore the present vogue for ladies tooling their own carriages.'

'Why not simply leave him here when you take Robina out?' her ladyship enquired, at a loss to understand why her son was making such an issue of an easily resolved problem.

His expression was faintly mocking. 'Because unlike you, Mama, who have proved to be possibly the most negligent chaperon on the face of the planet since we took up residence here in Brighton, I'm endeavouring to ensure that Robina's hitherto spotless reputation does not become slightly tarnished in the eyes of this censorious world of ours by being observed leaving the town's limits solely in my company.'

Although the explanation appeared to satisfy the Dowager, Robina was not quite so certain that she fully understood the reason behind his lordship's resolve to observe the proprieties wherever possible. Whose reputation was he striving to protect—hers or his own? she couldn't help asking herself. Was he doing everything within his power to ensure that she was not forced into a union with him? Or was he determined that he would not be obliged to offer her the protection of his name because of any gossip which might arise from their being observed together? And why was it, she wondered, had the latter possibility brought a return of that very uncomfortable hollow feeling deep inside?

By the time she had taken her place beside his lordship in the curricle later that morning, Robina had come very close to convincing herself that Daniel's determination to have a third person present as much as possible whenever in her company was prompted by entirely unselfish motives. Yes, she had almost convinced herself, but not quite.

She refused, however, to permit the remaining lingering little doubt to mar the pleasurable excitement she was experiencing at the prospect of being taught to handle such a fine pair of horses.

Having been expected to perform many tasks over the years under her mother's watchful eye had certainly stood her in good stead for just such an occasion as this, Robina reflected, happily taking charge of the equipage as they reached the outskirts of the town and the open countryside lay before them beckoning invitingly. At some point in her young life she had acquired a dogged determination not to allow fear of failure or an expert's critical opinion to prevent her from attempting something new. Consequently, she was able to concentrate fully on the task in hand, even though she had been forewarned that the small, stocky individual perched on the seat behind her was undoubtedly watching her every move, just waiting for the opportunity to give his opinion of 'uppity' females who thought themselves capable of handling the ribbons by giving vent to a loud snort at any foolish mistake she might make.

Thankfully no such derisive sound reached her ears. More satisfying still was the fact that only once, before she was requested to draw to a halt at a convenient spot in the lane where there was room enough for two carriages to pass quite comfortably, did her tutor feel the need to correct a slight error by placing his hand over hers, though why the fleeting and unexpected contact should have resulted in her heart momentarily beating a little faster she was at a complete loss to understand.

'That performance was extremely creditable for a person who has only before ever handled a one-horse gig,' Daniel announced, sounding genuinely impressed. 'What say you, Kendall?'

An ominous silence, then, 'Miss Perceval, m'lord, 'as a pair o' good light 'ands, I'll give 'er that.'

'Praise, indeed!' murmured Daniel for his pupil's ears only. Then louder, 'Do you wish to continue, or would you like me to take over now?'

Although highly delighted with her progress thus far, and with the praise she had received, even the groom's mild offering, Robina knew her limitations. Her arms felt a little tired, and her head was beginning to throb with the sheer effort of concentrating so hard, so she decided she'd had enough for one day and willingly handed back the reins.

'Do you wish to return to the house, or would

you, perhaps, enjoy a further exploration of the countryside?'

She certainly would have enjoyed that, but felt she ought not to impose on his lordship's good nature further by taking up any more of his time, and echoed her thoughts aloud.

'You are not imposing, I assure you,' he countered. 'If I hadn't wished to drive you about, child, believe me, I would never have offered.'

There was an undoubted glint in his eyes which in a child might have been taken for devilment. 'You appear to have gleaned, undoubtedly from my endearing mama, a very false impression of my character, my little bird. It is worth remembering that doting parents frequently refuse to see faults in their offspring.'

'Is that so, my lord?' Robina parried, a rare dry note creeping into her voice. 'In that case, all I can say is that you have been blessed, for my mama, loving and caring though she has unfailingly been throughout my life, has never been slow to point out my many failings.'

Having found himself in the punctilious Lady Elizabeth Perceval's company on numerous occasions during those weeks spent in London, and having become in recent years something of an astute judge of character, Daniel was not surprised by this innocent disclosure, but chose not to comment, and merely said,

'Besides which, I have a very good reason for pandering to your every whim. I am hoping that you will grant me a favour in return.'

He watched the questioning lift of delicate brows. 'You see, I've written to Miss Halliwell, my daughters' governess,' he explained, 'expressing my wish that she breaks the journey to Lyme Regis by spending a few days here in Brighton with us. My daughters, Hannah and Lizzie, spend a month each summer visiting their great-aunt Agatha in Dorset. She was my father's youngest sister and simply dotes on the girls.'

That lovely and totally spontaneous smile, which never failed to reach her eyes, and which was the very first thing he had ever noticed about Miss Robina Perceval, curled up the corners of that perfectly shaped mouth of hers.

'How delightful! I had secretly hoped that I might be given the opportunity of making your daughters' acquaintance. Lady Exmouth has told me so much about them that I feel I know them already.'

Daniel smiled to himself as he recalled that the second thing that had occurred to him about Robina in those first meetings in London was that she always managed to say precisely the right thing. She really was a darling!

'Well, I'm relieved to hear you say that, because I hoped you would assist me by keeping them amused whilst they're here. Lizzie, I'm afraid, is easily bored. It may well yet prove to be a grave error of judgement on my part, but I've tended to be rather indulgent since their mother's demise, and Lizzie, I'm afraid, can be something of a handful on occasions.'

It wasn't the admission itself which momentarily deprived her of speech, for she had learned from the Dowager that her son was both a loving and lenient father. It wasn't the fact that this was the first time, as far as she could recall, that he had ever mentioned his wife, either. What had come as a complete surprise was the fact that there had not been, as far as she could detect, so much as a hint of sadness in his deep, mellow voice.

She cast a fleeting sideways glance up at the strong contours of his wholly masculine profile to discover that, although he wasn't precisely smiling, there was nothing in his expression to suggest that mentioning his wife had caused him the least distress.

'Having three younger sisters myself, I can appreciate the mischief young girls can get into from time to time. I shall be only too happy to offer any assistance I can, my lord,' she assured him, and was surprised for the second time within the space of a few short minutes to discover that her willing offer of help did not appear to please him very much. In fact, if anything, he looked faintly annoyed.

The reason behind the unexpected frown was soon made clear. 'I thought we had agreed that we would dispense with formality when in private, Robina.'

'We did,' she agreed, unable to forbear a smile, or to resist the temptation to tease him a little. 'But might I remind you, sir, that we are not alone. Kendall is with us.'

Only for a moment did Daniel take his eyes off the road ahead to cast her a narrow-eyed, deeply assessing stare. 'I am beginning to realise that when my daughters arrive I shall have not just one unruly little baggage residing under my roof. Thank heavens my Hannah is always well behaved!'

Robina frankly laughed. She had been called many things in her young life, most notably a sweet, biddable girl, which in recent years she had found increasingly irksome. It always made her feel as if she were a complaisant half-wit, some mindless creature without a will of its own. So it was little wonder that his lordship's observation had come as something of a refreshing change, more like a compliment than any slur on her character, though she doubted very much that he had intended it as such.

Feeling marvellously content, a state which she had been experiencing very frequently of late, she leaned back in the comfortable seat and gazed about with interest at the unfamiliar landscape, something which she had not dared to do whilst tooling the curricle herself, lest she lose her concentration and make some foolish mistakes. His lordship, on the other hand, seemed quite capable of doing both. He really was most accomplished at handling the ribbons, controlling the spirited greys with effortless ease.

On the few occasions she had been privileged to sit beside him in the curricle, she had not once witnessed him give way to temptation with displays of dashing flair. He had never, for instance, attempted to feather-edge a corner or manoeuvre the curricle between two vehicles with only an inch to spare. She didn't doubt for a moment that he could easily accomplish such feats, but she could never imagine him putting either his horses or any passenger he might have taken up beside him at risk by making the attempt, unless the manoeuvres were totally unavoidable. Which made her ponder yet again on what must have occurred eighteen or so months ago that had resulted in the tragic accident which had killed his wife.

She was not so foolish as to suppose for a moment that only careless exhibitionists met with accidents. Where horses were concerned anything might happen at any time. Why, one only had to consider the many occasions her good friend Lady Sophia Cleeve, a fine horsewoman by any standard, had taken a tumble from her mount, or the occasional mishap her cousin Hugo, a most notable whip, had experienced over the years, to appreciate that the most skilful handlers of horseflesh could, and often did, come to grief from time to time. None the less she found it difficult to believe that a momentary lack of concentration or gross negligence on Daniel's part had resulted in the death of his much beloved wife.

It was all rather pointless trying to speculate on what might have occurred, she reminded herself. She had never been given any details about the accident whatsoever. Which, now she came to consider the matter, was most strange. The Dowager simply adored her son and never required much encouragement to begin talking about him.

From things she had let fall from time to time, her ladyship had been touchingly fond of her late daughter-in-law too. Whether the truth of the matter was simply that the Dowager wasn't in possession of all the facts herself, or that she found the subject of the beautiful Clarissa's demise too painful a topic to discuss, was anyone's guess. It was strange, all the same, that Lady Exmouth had never once attempted to touch on the subject.

Robina came out of her reverie to discover that they had, at some point, turned off the narrow twisting lane, and were now bowling along a much wider road and at a much brisker pace. From the position of the sun, she judged that Daniel had decided to head back to Brighton to enjoy the light luncheon which no doubt awaited their return. She was just beginning to feel that she could do justice to whatever the excellent cook had prepared for them, when she caught sight of a great deal of activity in a field just up ahead.

'Oh, what is taking place over there, do you suppose?'

'It'll be one of the horse fairs held in these parts every summer. The main one takes place in August.' He couldn't mistake the faint look of interest in her blue eyes. 'Would you care to stop and take a look? There are bound to be some sideshows.'

Robina very much looked forward to the annual summer fête held in the grounds at Perceval Hall, her uncle's estate in Northamptonshire. She would miss it this year, as it always took place in July, so she would not have minded in the least making up for the loss of that particular yearly treat by enjoying this unexpected event now. Nevertheless, always considerate to the feelings of others, she expressed her wish not to upset Cook by being late for one of her delicious luncheons.

'There's no need to concern yourself on that score,' Daniel assured her, after expertly turning the curricle into the field and quickly finding a sheltered spot beneath some trees. 'I made it clear before I left the house that I was unsure of precisely when we would return.'

'But what about Kendall?' Robina said, willingly accepting his lordship's helping hand to alight. She turned towards the groom, who now stood at the horses' heads. 'Do you not care to browse too?'

'No, thank you—er—Miss Robina. I'm more than 'appy to bide a while 'ere in the shade, and enjoy me pipe.'

Daniel cast a brief glance at his trusted henchman, before easily capturing Robina's hand, placing it in the crook of his arm, and leading her towards the first of the sideshows. She was perhaps sublimely unaware of it herself, but Kendall's familiarity had not been a token of disrespect, far from it. Robina had undoubtedly found favour in the loyal retainer's eyes.

'I rather fancy that Kendall was more impressed with your display this morning than he would have you believe, my little bird.' That and your undoubted consideration for the feelings of others, he added silently.

'I must confess I was rather pleased with my performance myself,' she admitted, smiling faintly as the thought occurred to her that, had her dear father been present to hear that particular disclosure, he would probably have approved of her honesty, but the self-gratification might well have earned her a frown of disapproval.

Evidently her present companion did not appear to think that she was being in any way conceited, for he smiled down at her like some indulgent uncle. He had a delightful smile; she had thought so from the first. It emphasised that rather attractive cleft in his firm chin, and crinkled the corners of those warm brown eyes.

'Yes, well,' she said faintly, amazed at her wayward thoughts, and fervently hoped that the sudden heat she could feel in her cheeks might be attributed to the warmth of the day. 'I do realise, of course, that I've still a great deal to learn. Tooling Papa's one-horse gig, with dear old Bessie between the traces is one thing; trying to control a pair of spirited horses is quite another.'

While she had been speaking, she had been taking a keen interest in the various attractions and the wide variety of wares for sale on the stalls, but now her sweet countenance unexpectedly betrayed a hint of distaste. Daniel followed the direction of her disapproving gaze to see a brightly coloured sign inviting people to step behind the screen to inspect the wondrous sight of a calf with two heads, a goose with three legs and various other oddities.

'Evidently you disapprove of such spectacles, child.'

'I find them distasteful in the extreme, not to mention needlessly cruel. Not many of those poor creatures are destined to live for very long. It would be much kinder to put them out of their misery at birth. On the other hand, though,' she sighed, 'who am I to criticise or condemn? I have never known hunger. I cannot truly blame any poor wretch for ensuring that his children have food in their bellies, no matter how distasteful the means by which he achieves this might be.'

Her smile swiftly returned as they reached the next attraction, a rough wooden structure housing, if the sign outside were to be believed, the world's fattest lady. Two yokels suddenly emerged from behind the screen, both, it appeared, decidedly unimpressed after witnessing the spectacle.

'She weren't as fat as the one they 'ad 'ere last year,' the taller remarked in a carrying voice, after fortifying himself from the jug he carried.

'No, she weren't,' his companion readily agreed. 'She weren't nearly so fat as your wife, come to that.'

'No, she weren't. I were thinking the selfsame—'Ere, what do you mean?' the first demanded, evidently realising at last what his friend had just said. 'I'll 'ave you know my Betsy ain't fat, just got plenty o' meat on the bone, that's all.' He fastened one grimy hand on his friend's shirt, spilling some of the contents of the jug in the process. 'You takes that back!'

Swiftly drawing his highly amused companion away before the ex-friends came to blows, which looked imminent, Daniel gazed down at her smiling face, thinking what a wicked sense of humour she possessed, something which he had suspected from the first.

He was convinced, too, that Lady Elizabeth Perceval had instilled strict codes of conduct in her eldest daughter, and this he considered highly commendable. He knew from experience that children needed to be kept under control and taught how to behave, as long as one remembered not to take discipline to extremes, and thereby run the risk of crushing a child's natural vivacity. He would not go so far as to say that this is what had happened in Robina's case, but he had felt increasingly, as he suspected his far from obtuse mother had too, that Robina had been reared to maintain a strict control over emotions and inclinations. She would no doubt always continue to do so to a certain degree, but since their arrival in Brighton there had already been a very noticeable change in her. She seemed far more relaxed and outgoing, and he couldn't help wondering how many more interesting facets of her character would emerge during the forthcoming weeks.

They continued their inspection of the stalls and sideshows, but none of the attractions, or the variety of gaudy fairings for sale, tempted Robina to untie the string of her reticule and part with the small quantity of money that Daniel did not doubt she carried with her. Only when they approached a brightly coloured caravan, with a sign on its door bidding one and all to enter and have their fortunes told by the all-seeing Madame Carlotta, did Robina hover for an instant, a wistful expression fluttering over her features before she made to move on.

'Go on,' he prompted. 'Why not indulge yourself?'

'Oh, no. I couldn't possibly do that. Papa would never approve. He considers all fortune-tellers charlatans.'

'Undoubtedly some of them are,' Daniel agreed, still gently preventing her from moving on. 'But any father who takes the trouble to teach his eldest daughter both Latin and Greek,' he continued, making use of a surprising fact he had discovered himself since their sojourn in Brighton, 'must surely consider her intelligent enough to form her own opinion, and would not, I feel certain, deny her the opportunity to do precisely that.'

Seemingly much struck by this viewpoint, she appeared to debate within herself. 'What harm can it do? Go along, child,' he urged again, and she finally gave way to temptation, quickly moving away before he had the opportunity to delve into his pocket for his purse and pay for the harmless experience.

Evidently the gypsy was a true professional, conveying her predictions with lightning speed, for in no time at all, it seemed, Robina was descending the caravan's steps, a look of wry amusement on her face.

'Let that be a lesson to me to attend my father in the future,' she announced, as she reached Daniel's side and, without the least prompting, slipped her arm through his. 'Papa was absolutely right, as he so often is—a fool and his money are soon parted!'

'You must allow me to pay. It was my suggestion, after all.'

'Certainly not!' she countered, retaining a firm hold on his arm, thereby preventing him from reaching for his purse without an undignified struggle. 'It will serve as a salutary lesson not to be so gullible in the future.'

'From that I infer you are not altogether pleased with what yours holds in store.'

'On the contrary, if what I have just been told is to be believed, it seems I am destined to enjoy a truly blessed existence. Madame Carlotta told me precisely what any girl would wish to hear.'

'Which is?' he prompted, unable to prevent a twitching smile at the wry cynicism.

'Oh, the usual highly improbable things—my path will very soon be crossed by a tall, handsome stranger. Both adventure and danger lie ahead.

Whatever that is supposed to mean! Madame Carlotta didn't choose to divulge any details for some reason. Now, what else did she tell me?' Her finely arched brows drew together for a moment. 'Ha, yes! Not too many weeks will pass before I will find myself married to the man of my dreams. Furthermore, I am to give birth within a year to the first of the three sons my husband and I are destined to have during our long and excessively happy life together.'

Daniel turned his head away, thereby concealing his expression of utter delight. Three sons, by gad! he mused. And here I would happily have settled for just one.

The future was beginning to look very rosy indeed!

Chapter Four

Although she most certainly did consider that she had been more than a little foolish to waste so much as a single penny of her small allowance on having her fortune told, Robina was destined to experience a change of heart before her second week in Brighton had drawn to a close, and was even to begin to wonder whether Madame Carlotta truly did possess the rare gift of second sight.

The week turned out to be a very hectic one, with many more people arriving in the town and many more visitors calling at the house. Invitations were received in increasing numbers, and in the middle of the week Lady Exmouth arranged the first of several small and informal parties she planned to hold that summer.

Well into middle age she might have been, but

the Dowager proved that she was certainly not behind the times by ensuring that the trio of musicians hired for the evening played a selection of waltzes.

Although the dance had nowhere near achieved universal acceptance, it was being performed increasingly at private functions. Nevertheless, woe betide any young woman embarking on her London début caught swirling about a room on a gentleman's arm. She might well be considered fast, thereby risking social ruin.

This, however, Robina considered, hardly applied in her case any longer. She had behaved with the utmost propriety throughout her Season in London, and as it was highly unlikely that she would ever be privileged to enjoy another, unless she married well, her reputation was hardly likely to suffer to any significant degree as a consequence of performing the *risqué* dance at a private function.

None the less, she was very well aware that her mama, not so complaisant, nor anywhere near as forward-looking, as the irrepressible Lady Exmouth, would have staunchly disapproved of her taking part. Surprisingly enough she didn't allow this fact to deter her. After a brief battle with her conscience, she agreed to partner Daniel, a gentleman who, she was swiftly beginning to realise, possessed the innate ability of persuading her to do precisely what she knew she really ought not to do.

The instant he placed one shapely hand lightly on her waist and captured her fingers gently in the other, Robina was reminded vividly of that morning when she had paid a visit to her very good friend Lady Sophia Cleeve at Berkeley Square, and had witnessed the dance performed for the very first time. It had been Sophia's intention to ask her brother to help demonstrate the steps. Unfortunately Lord Angmering had unexpectedly left town, and Sophia, never easily thwarted, had swiftly secured the services of her personal groom.

Robina had suspected at the time that her good friend had not been as indifferent to the handsome man swirling her about the elegant drawing-room in Berkeley Square as she had tried to appear, and that Sophia had been in a fair way to losing her heart. That the groom had turned out to be none other than the Duke of Sharnbrook was a fact known by very few; and although the fashionable world at large had been surprised by the speed of their engagement, no one who had attended the small, very select party, held at the Duke's ancestral home, had doubted for a moment that the newly betrothed couple were genuinely in love.

All this, of course, Robina was forced silently to concede, had little to do with the strange reaction she now found herself experiencing as Daniel expertly swirled her about the salon. It wasn't as if there had never been any physical contact between them either, she reminded herself. His lordship had never failed to offer a helping hand to get in and out of a carriage. Somehow, though, this experience felt completely different.

By the time Friday evening had arrived, and she found herself once again comfortably established in his lordship's well-sprung carriage, Robina had managed to convince herself that the peculiar fluttering in her breast and the increased pulse rate had been the result of nothing more disturbing than a natural nervousness at performing the waltz in public for the very first time, and had nothing whatsoever to do with her partner's prolonged and wholly masculine touch.

The explanation was reasonable enough as far as it went, but it could hardly account for the fact that, when her hand had been claimed a little later for a second waltz by a very charming male guest, she had experienced no reaction at all. She had decided, however, not to dwell on this very curious detail, and had succeeded up to a point in thrusting it from her mind.

She was very much looking forward to the evening ahead. It promised to be most enjoyable, not only because it would grant her the opportunity of furthering her acquaintance with several people she had met in London, but also because it meant that Lady Exmouth would be reunited with the hostess, a friend of many years standing, and one whom the Dowager had not seen for more than two decades.

'Am I correct in thinking that Lady Phelps, like yourself, has just one son?' Robina enquired when there was a lull in the conversation.

'Yes, that's right, dear. Just one of the many things we were destined to have in common throughout our lives.' Leaning back against the squabs, her ladyship quickly relapsed into a reminiscent mood. 'We took the matrimonial plunge within a month of each other, both marrying men much older than ourselves, and both sadly losing our husbands within weeks of each other. We were destined to have just the one child too, although Augusta had to wait many more years before her marriage was finally blessed. I have never met her son Simon, but am reliably informed that she simply dotes on the boy.'

'Lucky Simon,' his lordship remarked sardonically. 'I was little more than a poor, neglected waif, quite unloved.'

'Yes, and it shows, I'm afraid,' Robina responded, somehow managing to keep her countenance, unlike the Dowager, who offered her opinion of her son's grossly inaccurate remark by giving vent to a very unladylike snort.

'You were thoroughly spoilt. Your dear papa was nowhere near strict enough with you. Prematurely grey I went because of you, my boy! You were forever into mischief,' his own very loving mother declared. 'Still, I would far rather have had you that way than like poor Augusta's son. I gather he was something of a weak, sickly child, forever suffering from some ailment or other. That, I suppose, is one of the reasons why Augusta and I saw nothing of each other after Simon was born. That, and the fact that she married an Irish peer, and visits to England were, understandably, few and far between.'

'That and lack of funds, you mean,' his lordship corrected, revealing not for the first time in Robina's presence his streak of ruthless honesty. 'It is common knowledge that the late Lord Phelps was a dissolute rake and inveterate gambler. It was only his marriage to your friend Augusta Davenport that saved him from ruin.'

'True, I suppose,' her ladyship was forced to concede. 'From what I have gleaned from the letters Augusta and I have exchanged over the years, her son fortunately does not appear to have inherited his father's weaknesses. He spends most of his time painting and writing poetry, I believe.'

Daniel was decidedly unimpressed, as his expression clearly showed. 'Byron has a deal to answer for. Since the publication of Childe Harold every Tom, Dick and Harry fancies himself a dashed poet! Look at the rubbish we were forced to endure at Lady Tufnell's soirée in London. Never heard such a load of twaddle mouthed in one evening in my life!'

'Oh, it was not as bad as that, Daniel,' her ladyship countered. 'The trouble with you is that you completely lack a romantic soul. One or two of the offerings were most moving, don't you agree, Robina?'

'Unfortunately, ma'am, I find myself quite unable to offer an opinion.' There was just a suspicion of a twitch at the corner of her mouth. 'If my memory serves me correctly, on that particular occasion I was seated beside your son, and found my attention all too frequently straying in my attempts to prevent him from dropping off to sleep.'

The only response to this gentle teasing was a deep rumble of masculine laughter, a sound heard far more frequently of late, and one which was music to the Dowager's ears.

How glad she was now that she had used every ounce of self-control she possessed, going against her natural inclinations, and had not interfered in the developing relationship between her son and Robina, she reflected, turning her head to gaze sightlessly through the carriage window.

Anyone observing them together might be forgiven for supposing that a wonderful bond of friendship had developed between them. Which of course was precisely what had occurred. There was undeniably a genuine fondness on both sides, which was plain for anyone to see, but certainly no hint of any lover-like affection between them. Daniel treated Robina as he might have done some favoured younger sister, and Lady Exmouth very much suspected that Robina, in her turn, was beginning to look upon Daniel as the brother she had never been blessed to have.

She smiled to herself. Her son, with the patience and understanding that was so much a part of his nature, was being immensely cautious by slowly, very slowly, winning the regard of the woman he had chosen to marry. There wasn't the smallest doubt left now in Lady Exmouth's mind that her son truly did wish to marry the parson's daughter, though precisely why he was determined to do so was not quite so clear.

Unlike his first wife Robina was a very restful young woman, who always appeared sublimely content sitting with Daniel in companionable silence in the library or the parlour, reading her book. She was intelligent too, and was not afraid to venture an opinion on a great many important topics. On several occasions during the past two weeks the Dowager had come upon them when they had been debating some controversial issue, something which her ladyship could never recall Daniel ever doing with his first wife.

Yes, she mused, there wasn't the slightest doubt that they were admirably well suited. There wasn't the least doubt in her mind, either, that Daniel was managing to conceal the depth of his feelings, though whether he had, against all the odds, fallen in love for the second time in his life was a question which she was quite unable to answer.

The carriage drawing to a halt brought an end to the Dowager's pleasurable deliberations. She did not delay in alighting and leading the way into the house her childhood friend had taken for the duration of her stay in Brighton. She was very much looking forward to the reunion and, quite naturally, was prepared to find her friend vastly altered.

It just so happened, however, that it was not the first glimpse of Lady Phelps, now pale and gaunt, and looking every one of her five-and-fifty years, which almost brought Lady Exmouth to an abrupt halt in the doorway leading to the elegant drawing-room, but the sight of the blond-haired Adonis standing sentinel-like beside her.

Lady Exmouth was not so advanced in years that she could no longer appreciate a fine specimen of manhood. She had known numerous truly handsome gentlemen in her lifetime, and yet she could not bring one to mind to equal the young man standing before her now, bowing over her hand with seeming effortless grace. With his perfectly proportioned physique and a face whose features resembled those on some classic Greek statue, he might almost, she decided, be described as beautiful.

She tried to assess her protégée's reaction to such a rare specimen, but apart from a slight widening of those clear blue eyes, Robina betrayed no visible sign that the outstanding young man was having the least effect on her young heart.

The arrival of more guests ensured that exchanges of pleasantries were kept to a minimum, and Daniel, smiling a trifle wryly, shepherded the ladies further into the room. 'I am well aware that appearances quite frequently are deceptive, but I wouldn't have supposed for a moment that our young host suffers unduly from ill health.'

'No, indeed,' his mother agreed. 'Quite the contrary, I would have thought, unlike his poor mama. The years have been less than kind to dear Augusta. How thin and jaded she has become!' She turned to Robina. 'What did you think, my dear? Did you not find Lord Phelps excessively handsome?'

'Yes, very. And singularly lacking in conceit too, I noticed, which I rather admired.'

The Dowager nodded in agreement, secretly pleased by this response. She ought to have known that a sensible girl like Robina would not permit herself to be beguiled by a handsome face. 'And what is your opinion of the young man, Daniel?'

'I'm afraid, ma'am, I am a poor judge of masculine charms. Or lack of 'em, as the case may be,' he returned, taking a glance about him. 'Ha!

I see your faithful admirer is amongst the guests. If you'll excuse me…'

Was that a hint of impatience she had detected in his pleasantly mellow voice? Robina wondered, following his progress across the room. She didn't doubt for a moment that he, like anyone else, experienced it from time to time, and anger too, she supposed, though she had noticed precious little evidence of either during the time she had been privileged to know him.

She transferred her attention momentarily to the portly Baronet whose companionship Daniel had sought. A close friend of the Regent's and a long standing member of the so-called Carlton House set, Sir Percy Lovell had by all accounts been a serious contender for the Dowager's hand many years ago, and had remained a lifelong friend.

Robina had met him on several occasions during her Season in London, and again here when he had been amongst the guests at the Dowager's dinner party on Wednesday evening. She rather liked him herself, and wasn't in the least unhappy to find herself a short time later seated beside him at the highly polished table which had been prepared for the dozen or so privileged guests who had been invited to dine before the party officially got under way.

'I must say,' he remarked, helping himself to generous portions from several of the tasty dishes on offer, 'Augusta has arranged a decent spread here. Or her excellent cook was determined to display her skill.' His eyes momentarily strayed in their hostess's direction. 'By the looks of old Gussie she don't concern herself overmuch about food any more. Never was more shocked in my life than when I clapped eyes on her earlier! To look at her now you'd never believe she was a plump little pullet in her younger days. Still, the years bring some changes to all of us, I suppose.'

Robina could not forbear a smile at this. The years had certainly wrought changes in Sir Percy, if what she had been told was true. He had been, by all accounts, a fine figure of a man in his youth. Sadly this was no longer the case. A carefree bachelor existence and an undoubted weakness for the finer things in life had taken their toll on his physical appearance. His girth, according to the Dowager, had more than doubled in size during middle age, and his permanently high colour was testament to his love of fine old port and brandy.

'I think Lady Exmouth was slightly shocked by the changes she perceived in Lady Phelps too,' she divulged. 'But, as you remarked yourself, people are bound to change in two decades.'

'Lavinia hasn't to that extent. Put on a bit of weight in recent years, though, I suppose.' He glanced briefly at his own opulent midriff. 'Still, who hasn't?' He transferred his merry, round eyes, which, Robina was becoming increasingly aware, very little escaped, to the much slimmer form sitting at the head of the table. 'I must say young Phelps came as something of a surprise, also. Never would have supposed that Augusta, never much to look at even in her youth, and the late Lord Phelps could have produced such a handsome fellow.'

Unlike most of the other young ladies present, Robina had refrained from glancing too often at the head of the table, but did so now. 'He is without doubt the most handsome man I have ever met in my life,' she responded, betraying what she had thought when first setting eyes on the young lord. 'The mere sight of him is enough to send any young maiden's heart afluttering. He is still young, of course. Just four-and-twenty, I believe the Dowager said. I think when the time comes for him to marry, there will be no shortage of young ladies wishing to become his wife.'

'Mmm,' was the only response forthcoming before Sir Percy refreshed himself from the glass at his elbow.

'You do not agree, sir?'

'I wonder whether the next Lady Phelps will be entirely of his own choosing, m'dear.'

Robina was not slow to follow the Baronet's train of thought. Although Lady Phelps had greeted her warmly enough on her arrival, Robina had managed to detect a certain calculating look in the lacklustre eyes, and had wondered whether Lady Phelps's rather lethargic demeanour, like Sir Percy's frequently vague, childlike gaze, might well prove to be quite misleading.

'Would you be suggesting by any chance that he might be obliged to seek his mama's consent before he places a betrothal ring on any lady's finger?'

Sir Percy beamed approvingly. 'I suspected you were a clever little puss the very first time I met you,' he disclosed. 'Yes, m'dear, you have the right of it. That is precisely what I do think. I also think that she'll not be in too much of a hurry to give her consent, either.'

Robina was not granted the opportunity to comment further, even had she wished to do so, for the personable young gentleman seated on her left, a certain Mr Frederick Ainsley, whom she had met for the very first time that evening, claimed her attention.

It transpired that Mr Ainsley was actively seeking a career in the church. Consequently they had little difficulty in maintaining a conversation, and some little time had elapsed before Robina once again turned to the amiable Baronet to discover him working his way through a large portion of fresh strawberry meringue, liberally covered with large dollops of thick cream.

'Exmouth appears faintly subdued this evening,' he remarked, surprising her somewhat, and she quite naturally transferred her gaze momentarily to the place at the table where Daniel was seated, only to discover him looking directly back at her. She smiled, and for the first time ever won no answering smile, before he transferred his attention back to the lively damsel on his left.

'He was fine earlier. Quite jovial, in fact,' she divulged, clearly recalling the cheerful conversation during the short carriage journey. 'I suppose, though, past tragic events are bound to intrude into his thoughts, especially on an occasion such as this, when his wife would undoubtedly have accompanied him. I cannot imagine that one ever fully recovers from such a devastating blow, no matter how hard one might strive to do so.'

'Perhaps not,' Sir Percy conceded, after finishing the last morsel of delicious meringue on his plate, and with praiseworthy control not replacing it with a further helping. 'Clarissa was certainly a very sociable creature, much more so than Exmouth ever was. She loved to attend balls and parties, whereas Daniel is happiest when at home, looking after his estate.'

Sir Percy took a moment to fortify himself from his glass before continuing his interesting disclosures. 'Increasingly, as I recall, Clarissa would pay visits to London, staying with friends, or come here to Brighton, leaving Daniel back at Courtney Place to join her later. The marriage on the surface, though, appeared a happy one.'

Was that an element of doubt she had detected in his voice? Surely not! 'You knew the late Baroness very well, I presume.'

'Been a friend of the Exmouth family for years, m'dear. Yes, I knew her very well. She was exquisite. A diamond of the first water!' He stared down into the remaining contents of his glass, a slight frown puckering his wispy grey brows. 'Can't help thinking myself, though, that Exmouth married far too young. He'd only just attained the age of three-and-twenty, after all, and although he was always a very levelheaded young man, mature beyond his years, there's no trying to get away from the fact that the passage of time brings changes to us all, and not just physically.

'Clarissa, though, was outstandingly beautiful. No one could disagree with that. Would have succeeded in capturing any young man's heart. But there ain't much else you can do with a beautiful work of art except look and admire it, if you follow my drift. I don't mean to imply that she was a simpleton,' he added hurriedly, 'far from it, in fact, but her interests were a trifle limited, as you might say. Still,' he shrugged, 'as I've already mentioned, she seemed to suit young Exmouth well enough.

'Then came the accident,' he continued, while Robina was still digesting what he had already disclosed. 'All very tragic, as you've remarked yourself, m'dear. But something has always troubled me about it all… Something just never seemed quite right to me.'

Robina's interest was well and truly captured. 'Do you mean you were there at the time and witnessed the tragedy?'

'Oh, no, no! I was staying close by at the time, though, with a neighbour of Exmouth's. When news reached us, we jumped into the carriage and travelled over to Courtney Place. We learned then that Clarissa had died, and young John Travers, who had been paying a short visit to a maiden aunt residing nearby, had also been very badly injured in the accident. He never regained consciousness, poor fellow... Died the following day.'

Robina took a sip from her own glass, glancing across at Daniel as she did so. He was thankfully smiling now, that wonderful easy smile which he had so frequently bestowed upon her, while he happily conversed with the lively Lady Smethurst.

When she had first met him all those weeks ago in London, she had naturally felt saddened to learn about his bereavement, as much as one could experience sadness on hearing about the tragic loss suffered by a virtual stranger. Now, however, he was no longer a stranger, but her dear and wonderful companion whose friendship she had swiftly come to value far more than any other. Now the mere thought that he might be suffering hurt her unbearably too. It was almost a tangible thing, like a knife being thrust deep inside and cruelly twisted.

'When we arrived at Courtney Place, Daniel himself was not there,' Sir Percy went on to divulge, seemingly locked in the past. 'We were told he could be found at the scene of the accident, so we went along to see if there was anything we could do.' He shook his head sadly. 'Dreadful, it was. Clarissa's own carriage, the one Daniel had bought her the year before for her own private use, twisted and broken, lying at the bottom of the ravine, with the horses, both of which Daniel himself had shot to put an end to their suffering, lying alongside it.'

'What was it precisely about the accident which puzzled you, Sir Percy?' Robina prompted when he fell silent again.

'The location, m'dear,' he didn't hesitate to enlighten her. 'It happened on a stretch of road known locally as Snake Pass, for obvious reasons. It's a picturesque little run, but seldom used nowadays, not since the new road was constructed, except by farmers and sightseers, and then only during the summer months. It's virtually impassable during winter, and dangerous too. It follows the line of the hillside, and weaves in and out, hence its name.'

'Well?' she prompted again, determined to discover precisely what troubled him about the incident.

'Well, m'dear…I can't help asking myself what an intelligent man like Daniel was doing tooling his wife's carriage along a road he knew to be highly dangerous. Furthermore, I discovered that he had returned from London a matter of only an hour or two before the accident occurred. It just isn't the act of a sensible man to go gadding about, tooling a carriage, when one must surely be quite weary already after travelling from London.

'And sightseeing...?' he continued, deliberately keeping his voice low so that the conversation could not be overheard. 'Who in his right mind goes gadding about sightseeing on a filthy day in late October? Answer me that if you can! I clearly remember that it had been raining all that morning, and although the afternoon was dry, it was dull, damp and thoroughly dismal. Daniel informed me that it had been young Travers's idea. He had been keen to see something of the county before he returned to his home in Derbyshire. Well, I suppose that's feasible enough,' he conceded. 'But what I cannot swallow is that Daniel accepted the wager in the first place.'

'Wager?' Robina echoed, not clearly understanding what Sir Percy had meant.

'Seemingly, m'dear, young Travers suggested that any man who considers himself a capital whip ought to be able to tool a carriage competently in any weather, in any conditions and with reasonable speed. Exmouth certainly doesn't lack skill when it comes to tooling a carriage. You know that from experience yourself.' He shrugged his plump shoulders again. 'I'm not suggesting that he would never accept a wager—gentlemen do from time to time. But he would never have put his horses at risk, let alone his wife, by tooling a vehicle along that particular stretch of road. That to me totally lacks the ring of truth!'

Indeed it does, Robina silently agreed. Daniel would never do such a foolhardy thing, least of all for a wager. Sir Percy was right—it just didn't ring true somehow.

Later that night, as she climbed into bed, Robina was to recall again the conversation she had had with Sir Percy over dinner. It had proved most enlightening and had provided much food for serious thought.

That conversation was by no means the only interesting aspect of what had turned out to be a most enjoyable evening, she reflected, snuggling between the clean sheets. She had very much enjoyed the company of Mr Frederick Ainsley and had danced with him twice during the evening. The only slight disappointment was that Daniel hadn't once offered to lead her out on to the floor. The devastatingly handsome Lord Phelps most certainly had, though, making her feel the envy of every other young female in the room, and the cynosure of all eyes.

She frowned suddenly, as a thought suddenly occurred to her. The gypsy woman at the fair had predicted that a handsome young man would cross her path in the near future. And one most definitely had! The odd thing was, though, the experience of dancing with Lord Phelps had had little effect upon her, unlike two nights before, when Daniel had expertly guided her about the floor.

How very odd that was!

Chapter Five

The following morning it seemed to Robina that the door-knocker was never still. The first caller to the house was Mr Frederick Ainsley, who came for the sole purpose of inviting her to take a walk with him in the park. Ordinarily she would have been delighted to comply, but as she had already arranged with Daniel to go out with him in the curricle later that morning, a treat she would never willingly forgo unless wholly unavoidable, she politely declined, although she was more than happy to agree to the suggestion that they enjoy a promenade together the following afternoon.

No sooner had the very amiable Mr Ainsley taken his leave than their hostess of the previous evening, accompanied by her son, arrived at the house. The cruel light of day did little to improve

Lady Phelps's world-weary appearance, unlike her sole offspring's. Seating himself beside Robina on the sofa, he resembled some golden Apollo with the sun's rays streaming through the parlour window, enhancing the bright guinea-yellow of his curls.

Daniel, who had retired to his library directly after breakfast in order to write a long letter in response to the one he had received that morning from his steward, must have detected the sound of the door-knocker this time, for he joined them a few moments later. The conversation quickly turned to the present vogue in paintings, and other works of art, a subject on which, Robina had discovered the night before, the young Lord Phelps proved most knowledgeable. Daniel promptly enquired whether his young visitor would care to accompany him into the library to inspect the fine landscape hanging above the hearth. The invitation was speedily accepted, though whether it was a desire to view the painting which prompted the eager acceptance or Daniel's suggestion that they might partake of something rather stronger than the tea which the butler was at that moment carrying into the room, Robina was not perfectly sure.

Lady Exmouth was not slow to note the secretive little smile hovering about the sweet mouth of the young woman whom she very soon hoped to call daughter, and couldn't help wondering precisely what was passing through that quick little mind. Her ladyship was nothing if not a realist, and was very well aware that the unexpected arrival of such a handsome young man on the scene might well give rise to some unforeseen problems, so it was with some satisfaction that she noted that her young protégée did not appear in the least downcast at having the young Adonis removed from her sphere.

Unlike Robina, Lady Phelps watched the gentlemen leave the room and waited for the door to be firmly closed behind them, before turning to her friend and offering her condolences on the death of Daniel's wife. 'Simply a dreadful tragedy. Clarissa was such a beautiful girl! So full of life, as I remember.'

'Indeed she was,' Lady Exmouth agreed, handing her visitor a filled china cup. 'Daniel, thankfully, is recovering well. His weeks in London did him a great deal of good.'

Lady Phelps's dull grey eyes flickered momentarily in Robina's direction. 'I'm pleased to hear it. He is still a relatively young man, not yet six-and-thirty, if my memory serves me correctly. He must not be allowed to mourn forever.'

She turned her eyes once again in Robina's direction, only this time her gaze was considerably more direct. 'And you, my dear, are you enjoying your stay in Brighton?'

'Very much so, ma'am. Both Lady Exmouth and her son have been so very kind.'

'Nonsense, child! It's a joy having you with us. Male company is all very well for a time, but one still needs the companionship of one's own sex. Robina is the eldest daughter of Lady Elizabeth Finedon, that was, and William Perceval, Augusta,' Lady Exmouth explained, after she had finished dispensing the tea.

'Ha, yes! Yes, of course. Your papa is a clergyman, is that not so, my dear?'

'Yes, ma'am. He is the Vicar of Abbot Quincey.'

'A worthy gentleman, I'm sure. I remember your mama very well. You have younger brothers and sisters, I presume.'

'Three sisters.'

'How very lucky your parents are! I was only blessed with the one child.' She turned to her friend. 'But we have been most fortunate in our children, Lavinia, have we not?'

'Very. And Simon is such a very handsome young man, Augusta!'

Lady Phelps permitted herself a thin smile. 'But, alas, never strong.'

This brought a faint flicker to one corner of the Dowager's mouth, Robina noticed. No doubt her ladyship thought, as she did herself, that Lord Phelps looked the very picture of health, with his fresh complexion, clear, sparkling eyes and shining crop of guinea-gold curls.

Although the Dowager had certainly not admitted to it in so many words, Robina had gained the distinct impression that the reunion had not turned out to be quite the joyful occasion for which Lady Exmouth had hoped. From odd little snippets she had let fall during the carriage ride home the previous evening, it was quite evident that she considered that her old friend had changed out of all recognition in many ways, and not for the better. Robina remembered too the look she had glimpsed on the Dowager's face when her ladyship and Lady Phelps had been seated together on the sofa, enjoying a dish of tea after the delicious dinner served the previous evening. Robina had thought she had detected a hint of impatience in the Dowager's eyes, and a touch of boredom too.

There was no hint of boredom now, merely suppressed amusement, as she said, 'All children become ill from time to time. It's unavoidable, Augusta. I'm sure Simon cannot cause you concern, now, however. He looks the very picture of health.'

'Ah, but looks can be deceptive, my dear. He is nowhere near as robust as he might appear. And he carries a great deal of responsibility on those young shoulders of his. It is no secret that the estate came to him in a sorry state. Thankfully Simon has not inherited his father's weaknesses, and things are much improved.' The woebegone expression was noticeably more marked. 'It is still necessary, however, for Simon to marry well.'

'In that case, Augusta,' her ladyship returned bluntly, 'I cannot imagine what on earth prompted you to come here to Brighton. The real prizes are to be captured during the London Season.'

Lady Phelps's trill of laughter sounded more than a little forced. 'Oh, no, my dear! We did not come here with the intention of finding Simon a suitable wife. He is still very young, and has no intention of taking the matrimonial plunge quite yet. Of course, if he did happen to meet the right sort of girl, and fall in love, all well and good, but we really came to enjoy a change of scenery and take advantage of the healthy sea air.'

This in all probability was quite true, for the widow, at least, looked as though she could do with recouping her strength. The lady might not be in prime physical condition, but Robina didn't suppose for a moment that she lacked ambition, or cunning, come to that, and couldn't help wondering whether Lady Phelps would willingly allow a golden opportunity to ensnare a rich prize for her son to slip through her bony, mercenary fingers, if a suitable heiress did happen to arrive on the scene during their stay in Brighton.

Whether or not Lord Phelps himself wholeheartedly approved of these plans for his future, Robina had no way of knowing. As the days passed, and she found herself in his company quite frequently, unavoidable in a town such as Brighton, where the same people were continually invited to the same social events, she swiftly came to the conclusion that he was a remarkably complacent young man, with few ambitions, and few interests outside those of poetry and art.

He certainly never appeared particularly interested in pursuing any masculine outdoor activities, and seemed quite content to accompany his mother wherever she wished to go: social events in the evenings; about the town during the day to visit her friends. Not surprisingly they were regular visitors to Lord Exmouth's home, and it didn't take Robina very long to notice that their arrival at the house usually signalled Daniel's immediate departure from it.

Consequently she began to see far less of him. Lady Phelps's frequent calls were by no means solely responsible for this. July's arrival had brought a further influx of visitors to the town, which included good friends of Robina's from Northamptonshire, Olivia Roade Burton and her recently married sister Beatrice and her new husband, the very charming Lord Ravensden. Her visits to the Ravensden household, and her growing friendship with Frederick Ainsley who, unlike Lord Phelps, was fond of fresh air and regular exercise, ensured that Robina was frequently away from the house too.

Daniel's very good friend Montague Merrell also arrived in town, and quite naturally Daniel was keen to spend time with him, pursuing wholly masculine interests. Understandably enough, he did not always make himself available to squire Robina and his mother out in the evenings. This in itself caused no particular problems, except that Robina did miss him, a circumstance that she was not prepared to admit to until she was forced to do precisely that, when Daniel, one morning over breakfast, unexpectedly announced his intention of moving in temporarily with his friend Mr Merrell.

'For heavens' sake why, Daniel?' the Dowager responded, voicing Robina's particular thoughts very succinctly.

'It may have slipped your memory, Mama, but your grandchildren are due to arrive today.'

'Well? What of it? We've room enough to house them very comfortably. There's absolutely no need for you to move out.'

'Perhaps not,' he conceded, glancing at Robina, who was staring fixedly at the letter she had been reading, and had placed neatly beside her plate, 'but it would make things a deal more comfortable for you all if I do. Added to which, I flatly refuse to house Miss Halliwell in one of the attic rooms. She has been a constant comfort and support to the girls since their mother's death, and I will not have her treated like a servant. Hannah and Lizzie can share my room, and Miss Halliwell can occupy the one next door.'

Evidently the Dowager fully appreciated the kind consideration he was displaying towards his daughters' governess, and after a moment's deliberation she nodded in agreement.

'Good. That's settled then,' he responded, considering the matter now closed, and turned to Robina, who remained thoughtfully staring down at the letter by her plate. 'You're very quiet this morning, child. I trust your mother's missive brought no bad news?'

'W-what…? Oh, no. Not at all. Just a little local gossip. My family are eagerly awaiting the arrival of my cousin. She may already have arrived by now, of course.'

Robina forced herself to look at him, hoping the acute disappointment she was experiencing at his imminent removal from the house did not show in her face. 'You may remember I told you that Mama offered Cousin Deborah a home after her mama, my aunt Frances, passed away last year. I dare swear the vicarage will never be quite the same again once she takes up residence there. Darling Deborah has an unfortunate tendency to be—how shall I put it?—slightly accident-prone on occasions.' She glanced briefly at the letter once again. 'But apart from that, Mama only writes briefly that no one has been charged with Sywell's murder as yet.'

'It may well turn out to be one of those cases that never does get solved,' Daniel suggested, after a moment's thought. 'Although, from what Merrell was telling me t'other day, Prinny seems keen to have the thing cleared up.'

Lady Exmouth frowned at this. 'Why is that, do

you suppose? Sywell was never a close friend of the Regent's, surely?'

'From what I can glean, the Marquis wasn't anybody's friend,' Daniel returned, his dry sense of humour coming to the fore. 'No, that isn't it. It's simply that Prinny ain't too happy when he discovers that a member of the peerage has been—er—bumped off. There's been enough of that going on in recent years across the Channel. Our future king don't want anything of that sort starting here, and I can't say I blame him. Can't have gangs of revolutionaries going about bumping off our aristos, now can we? It might be my turn next!'

'I am the only person likely to murder you, my boy, for deserting me in this fashion!' his mother retorted. 'Thank goodness I still have dear Robina to bear me company. I'm seriously considering persuading her to return with me to Bath, after the summer, to be my constant companion. She, I am persuaded, would never desert me!'

'If you are not very careful, Mama,' Daniel warned, his smile slowly fading, and his gaze unusually intense, 'you might succeed in persuading her to do just that.'

As Daniel's time was taken up with organising the removal of some of his more personal belongings to take with him to his temporary lodgings, Robina had of necessity to forgo her lesson in the curricle that morning. She remained in the house with the Dowager, receiving the steady stream of morning callers, a regular feature of the past few days, but after luncheon was determined to go out for a breath of fresh air, and was delighted when Mr Frederick Ainsley arrived on the doorstep just as she was about to set forth, and offered to accompany her.

Only just of average height and, with the possible exception of a pair of clear, intelligent grey eyes, having no looks worthy of note, Mr Ainsley might not have been to every female's taste. Unlike Lord Simon Phelps, who gained attention wherever he went, Mr Ainsley could attend a party of an evening and most other guests present might never recall his being there, and yet Robina much preferred his company to the handsome young Earl's.

His many wonderful qualities, Robina considered, more than compensated for any lack of striking physical attributes. He was very much the gentleman, both courteous and attentive. He was intelligent too, and a most interesting conversationalist, unlike Lord Phelps who seemed to drift off at a moment's notice into a world of his own, leaving Robina with the distinct impression that he had not heard a single word that she had said.

Robina found that time always passed remarkably quickly whenever she was with Mr Ainsley. This occasion proved no exception, and she arrived back at the house rather later than she had intended to discover the butler in the process of organising the swift removal of the variety of baggage which littered the hall. Therefore she wasted no time in going up to her room to remove her bonnet, and tidy her hair, and then went straight down to the front parlour to discover, as expected, Daniel's daughters sitting with their grandmother on the sofa, and a female in a plain grey gown seated nearby in one of the comfortable chairs.

Daniel himself was also present. He rose to his feet the instant she entered the room, and greeted her with, 'Ha! So the wanderer returns at last,' which might well have been meant as criticism. If it was he tempered it with a welcoming smile, and a raised hand beckoning her forward.

'Miss Perceval, permit me to present my daughters, Hannah and Elizabeth.'

Although she and her three sisters might differ slightly in looks, there could be no mistaking their close relationship. The same could not be said for the two girls who now stood before her, executing curtseys with differing skills. Hannah, with her dark hair and soft brown eyes, certainly favoured her father in looks; whereas Lizzie, Robina suspected, was bidding fair to becoming the image of her lovely mother, having a pair of limpid blue eyes and a riot of bright guinea-gold curls.

She swiftly discovered that they were vastly different in temperament too. Hannah, seeming older than her twelve years, was quiet and refined; whereas Lizzie, it quickly became apparent, possessed all the boundless energy of a nine-year-old child, wanting always to be on the move. Her father, however, managed to persuade her with very little difficulty to sit quietly beside her grandmother once again, while he introduced Miss Halliwell.

Robina's experience of governesses was limited. Private tutors were luxuries her parents could ill afford, and she and her sisters had received their education at the vicarage from their parents, both of whom were highly intelligent and well read. There had been one or two governesses residing in the locale over the years, and of course her good friend Lady Sophia Cleeve had received private tuition from several different females during her formative years, all of whom, as far as Robina could remember, had been cast in a similar mould: gaunt, bespectacled and middle-aged. Miss Halliwell certainly did not conform to this stereotype, for she was, Robina judged, only in her mid to late twenties, and was very attractive, with a slim, shapely figure.

'Before you joined us,' Daniel said, once again seating himself after Robina had done so, 'we were discussing what we could do tomorrow to entertain the girls. Have you any ideas?'

'Well, if the weather remains fine,' she responded, after giving the matter a moment's thought, 'and it shows every possible sign of doing so, we might go into the country somewhere and have a picnic.'

The suggestion gained immediate approval from both girls, and Hannah in particular, who was keen to take her sketching pad to record the local scenery.

'That's settled then,' her father said indulgently. 'All that remains is for us to decide precisely where we are to enjoy this alfresco luncheon. Any thoughts on that score, Miss Perceval?'

Robina felt certain that her cheeks were growing quite pink with the warmth of the smile he cast her, and she could only hope that the added bloom might be deemed to be the quite natural outcome of her recent walk in the fresh air.

'There is that very pretty wooded area we passed when you took me into the country for my very first lesson in the curricle. It is situated very near where they hold the horse fairs,' she explained when he frowned in puzzlement. 'I seem to remember you said there was a ruined priory somewhere nearby, which I should imagine would make an ideal subject for sketching.'

'Ha, yes! I know where you mean. There were always several pairs of swans on the river there, as I recall.' She received a further warm smile of approval. 'Clever girl that you are, Miss Perceval, you have come up with the ideal spot—sufficient shade for Mama if it becomes too warm, and a wood for the more energetic amongst us to explore.'

'Have you been teaching Miss Perceval to tool your curricle, Papa?' Hannah enquired, resembling her father more closely still when she frowned. 'I cannot recall your ever teaching Mama.'

'Your mama never betrayed the least interest to learn, unlike Miss Perceval who continually astounds me by betraying a surprising interest in a wide range of things.'

'Will you teach me, Papa?' Lizzie asked, wide-eyed and eager.

'Perhaps. When you're a little older. And providing you can learn to sit still for more than two minutes at a time,' he teased gently, rising to his feet as the tea-tray arrived in the room. 'In the meantime, we shall leave your grandmama to enjoy her refreshments in peace, while we go out and enjoy ices and lemonade.'

'Am I right in supposing that you herald from this part of the country, Miss Halliwell?' the Dowager remarked, after her son and granddaughters had left the room.

'Yes, that is correct, my lady,' she responded in a well-spoken voice.

'I seem to recall, too, your mentioning that you still have relatives residing hereabouts.'

'Yes, my lady. My brother and his family. My brother teaches in a school situated about five miles from Brighton.'

'In that case, my dear, why not take the opportunity whilst you're here of paying them a visit. In fact, why not spend the entire day with them tomorrow?' she suggested. 'My son would not object, I'm sure, to your making use of the chaise. We can easily manage with the travelling carriage.

And I shall not be at all surprised if Exmouth decides to drive himself in the curricle.'

It was quite obvious by the sudden expression of delight that Miss Halliwell wished to accept the kind offer, and equally obvious that she was not one to neglect her duties when she said, 'But surely you will wish me to accompany you tomorrow in order to take care of the girls?'

'I'm certain that we can manage quite well. Miss Perceval has three younger sisters, and is quite accustomed to keeping young ladies entertained. So, we'll take it as settled.'

The Dowager smiled at Robina, as she requested her to pour out the tea, and then turned back to the governess. 'By the by, my dear, you and Miss Perceval have more in common than your ability to keep a watchful eye on young girls. Like yourself, Miss Perceval is the daughter of a clergyman.'

The conversation quite understandably turned to the busy and pleasant life to be had in a country vicarage. It transpired that Miss Halliwell had lost her mother some years before, and had been expected at a young age to take upon herself the duties of managing the household. When her elder brother had left the family home in order to pursue his chosen career as a teacher, she had remained with her father, until his demise four years ago, when the living had quickly been offered to another and she had found herself without a roof over her head. She had chosen to enter the same profession as her brother, and had been fortunate enough to find employment within a very short space of time in the Exmouth household.

After listening to this brief history of Miss Halliwell's life, Robina began to realise fully, for perhaps the first time, just how much she had taken for granted over the years, and how privileged her own life had been compared to that of the vast majority of clergymen's offspring. Unlike the late Mr Halliwell, her own father had been able to afford the luxury of employing servants to attend to the heavier household chores. She had not been asked to clean and cook, or lay fires. Nor had she been expected to grow an ample supply of vegetables in order to save a little money, as Miss Halliwell had been forced to do.

Furthermore, how many clergymen's daughters could boast to having enjoyed a Season in London? How many had found themselves sitting in a titled gentleman's parlour, dispensing cups of tea, as though they were mistress of the house and had every right to do so, just as she was doing now?

She had adapted so easily to this privileged way

of life that she might have been born to it, which of course she had not. For the past few months, she told herself, she had been enjoying a fairytale existence, and it was high time she ceased her foolish dreaming and faced reality. If she returned to Abbot Quincey without receiving any further offers for her hand, she might well find herself having to seek some genteel employment in the not too distant future. After all, she could not expect her parents to support her indefinitely, and life as a governess might one day loom large on her own horizon. Miss Halliwell, it had to be said, seemed very contented with her lot. But how many governesses were lucky enough to find employment in the home of such a kind and considerate gentleman as Lord Exmouth? Precious few, Robina suspected.

Chapter Six

It was a merry little group which gathered in the hall late the following morning. Miss Halliwell had departed an hour or so earlier, with Lord Exmouth's full approval, to spend the day with her brother and his family. Robina, who had already managed to win the new visitors' stamp of approval, most especially Lizzie's, who was beginning to think that in Miss Perceval she might have found something of a kindred spirit, was successfully keeping the girls in a high state of amusement by recounting yet another of her less than commendable childhood exploits, when the front door opened and Daniel entered the house. To the little gathering's surprise he was swiftly followed by the ample form of Sir Percy Lovell, wearing a wide-brimmed straw hat and sporting a garish yellow-

and-green striped waistcoat, with a preposterously large nosegay tucked in his lapel.

'Great heavens!' her ladyship exclaimed, her gaze alternating between flowers and waistcoat. 'What in the world brings you here, Percy? Surely you're not to make up one of the party?'

'Most certainly am,' he assured her. 'When I ran across Exmouth last night, and he mentioned he was off on a jaunt into the country, I decided I wasn't prepared to miss out on the treat if I could help it, and so I invited myself.'

It was quite apparent that neither Hannah nor Lizzie, who joyfully greeted him, objected to his company. Sir Percy, beaming like some highly indulgent great-uncle, promptly presented Hannah with the nosegay, telling her that she was turning into a devilishly pretty gel, before informing Lizzie that she was a naughty little puss who ought to be kept on leading-strings, which only succeeded in making her chuckle and dance about him all the more.

'You are an appalling influence, Percy,' Lady Exmouth informed him, before casting a playfully accusing glance in quite another person's direction. 'But you are by no means the only one.'

Daniel, having instructed the footman to place a clean rug in his curricle, turned in time to overhear these latter remarks. 'Is that so!' he announced, slanting a look of mock severity directly upon the miscreant.

The only response forthcoming was a wickedly provocative blue-eyed glance which instantly produced a smile of such loving tenderness to transform his lordship's features that Sir Percy, blinking several times, stood transfixed.

The full import of what he was witnessing quickly permeated his brain. He was very well aware of course of precisely where his good friend the Dowager considered her son's future lay or, to be more precise, with whom. Nonetheless up until that moment he had not fully appreciated just how successful she had been in her endeavours. He glanced in her direction for confirmation, only to discover her making a great play of searching through her reticule, an unmistakable smile of satisfaction tugging at the corners of her own mouth.

'By Jove! Yes—er—well. Shall we be on our way?' he suggested, turning to lead the way outside.

Quite understandably both the girls had wished to travel in the curricle with their father. He was in the process of offering them a helping hand to scramble up on to the seat, when a lone horseman, trotting down the street in their direction, happened to catch his attention.

There was no hint of tenderness in the glance he directed at Robina this time. She looked as surprised as everyone else by the rider's approach, and her ladyship hurriedly stepped into the breach before her son's evident annoyance prompted him to say something which he might later come to regret.

'Why, good morning, Lord Phelps,' she greeted him, when at last he drew level with the small cavalcade. 'I sincerely trust you did not intend to pay us a morning call, for as you can see we are just about to depart for a jaunt in the country.'

'Yes, ma'am, I know. Hoped I might catch you before you left. Discovered earlier from my mother that you were organising a sketching party, and decided I'd come along. If you've no objection, that is?'

'Why, of course not,' she announced, with as much enthusiasm as she could muster, while hoping her slightly raised voice would conceal Sir Percy's string of muttered oaths. 'I'm certain Cook will have provided us with ample provisions.'

'What on earth possessed you to permit that fellow to tag along, Lavinia?' Sir Percy demanded, climbing into the coach after the ladies, and slamming the door firmly closed in case the new arrival should take it into his head to leave his mount and request a seat in the carriage. 'Damned impertinence turning up like that, and virtually inviting himself!'

'Well, that's rich coming from you!' she retorted. 'You did precisely the same thing yourself.'

'Ah, but that's different. I'm an old friend of the family. Knew you'd have no objection to me making up one of the party.'

'And what makes you suppose that I've the least objection to Lord Phelps doing precisely the same thing?'

'Should have thought that was obvious, m'dear,' he muttered, casting a meaningful glance at the sole occupant of the seat opposite, who had remained interestedly staring out of the window from the moment the carriage had moved off. 'Daniel wasn't best pleased. Any fool could see that.'

'Oh, I don't supposed he minded to any great extent,' she countered, not making the least attempt to lower her own voice. 'Why should he, for heaven sakes! Lord Phelps is quite harmless, you know.'

'Hopeless, maybe!' Then, again in an undertone, 'But devilish handsome.'

'Undeniably so.' The Dowager then decided to prove to her old friend that his obvious concerns were quite without foundation, and turned at once to Robina. 'Did you notice the look on Hannah's face, dear, when Lord Phelps came trotting down the street towards us?'

Robina could not forbear a smile. 'I did as it happens. I wish I had a shiny golden guinea for every occasion I'd glimpsed that particular expression since the young Earl arrived in Brighton. I'd be a very rich woman by now!'

'I cannot recall your gaping at him in just such a fashion when you were first introduced.'

Robina's eyes twinkled with amusement. 'That is because I had been forewarned, you see. A gypsy accurately predicted, as things have turned out, that a handsome man would cross my path.'

'Good heavens!' Lady Exmouth betrayed genuine surprise, and not just mild interest too. 'I did not realise you'd been to a fortune-teller, child. When did you go? Was it recently?'

'Yes, quite recently. When Lord Exmouth took me out for my very first lesson in the curricle, we came upon a horse fair and decided to take a look around. The fortune-teller was amongst the attractions.'

'How very exciting! What else did she tell you, my dear?'

Robina felt that she had been dwelling rather more than she should of late on what that gypsy woman had told her, secretly hoping, she supposed, that perhaps more than just one of the predictions might come true. It would be comforting to think that she was destined to enjoy a full and happy life, but she was desperately striving to be sensible about it all.

'Oh, not very much, ma'am.' She shrugged. 'One must not take these things too seriously.'

'She was certainly right about the handsome young man,' her ladyship pointed out, slightly disappointed by Robina's distinct lack of enthusiasm. 'Did she predict a marriage for you, by any chance?'

'Bah!' Sir Percy interjected rudely, thereby earning himself an impatient glance from his friend. 'Well, it's all stuff and nonsense, Lavinia, as you very well know. And if she did happen to predict a marriage for the gel, I hope to high heaven it wasn't to that buffoon riding alongside us.'

It was an effort but the Dowager did manage to suppress the chuckle rising in her throat. 'Now, that is unkind, Percy. I wouldn't suggest for a moment that Lord Phelps is a stimulating orator, but he certainly isn't a simpleton.'

'Seems one to me. Have you ever tried to hold a conversation with the halfwit? Why, he goes off into a world of his own at the drop of a hat. Still,' he shrugged, 'I suppose he has been forced to adopt such tactics in order to get away from that mother of his, if only to mentally distance himself,' he continued, striving to be fair. 'She never leaves the boy alone. Drags him about with her everywhere.'

'Yes, I had noticed that myself,' the Dowager was forced to concede.

'And I'll tell you another thing,' he went on, warming to the subject. 'Don't let those die-away airs of Augusta's fool you. She's as sharp as a razor, that one! And as mean as a moneylender to boot! I've had it on the best authority that the only reason she's in Brighton now is because she hasn't had to dip into her own purse to pay for the house she's staying in. It was her sister who hired it originally. Only when the sister became ill late in the spring, she offered it to Augusta. She snapped up the chance by all accounts. And hasn't paid her sister a penny piece, if I know anything!'

Lady Exmouth had not heard this particular tale, but wouldn't have been in the least surprised to discover it was true. 'I'm afraid Augusta has changed. She isn't the friend I remember.'

'Very true. So you be careful, m'dear,' Sir Percy warned. 'I've also heard a rumour that she intends to stay over in England until next year. The family no longer owns a property in this country, so I wouldn't put it past her to sponge off her friends. If you're not very careful, she'll be inviting herself to Bath in the autumn and inflicting her company on you.'

'She'll be out of luck if she tries,' her ladyship responded. 'My plans are still uncertain. I should like to return to Bath after the summer, but there is every chance that I shall be returning to Courtney Place with Daniel.'

Sir Percy did not attempt to hide his astonishment. 'Why on earth are you considering doing that? Daniel's fully recovered—happier than I've seen him look for years.'

'Do you really think so?' The Dowager was much struck by this. She valued Sir Percy's opinion more than he realised. 'Perhaps, then, there'll be no need for me to return to Kent.'

'No need whatsoever,' he assured her. 'I'll admit I thought he could do with your support after the accident happened. That's why I took it upon myself to travel to Bath to collect you.'

'And very grateful I was too,' she responded, casting him a fond smile.

'Well, it was little enough at the time.' He shook his head at the all too vivid memory. 'But as I've said, Exmouth's fully recovered now and more than capable of arranging his own future, Lavinia, old girl. So, if you take my advice, you'll allow him to do so. He'll not thank you for interfering,' he added, casting her a meaningful glance.

Robina, who had sat quietly digesting everything that had been said, was of a similar opinion. She wasn't so certain as Sir Percy appeared to be that Daniel had fully recovered from the tragedy of losing his lovely wife, but she was sure that he was more than capable of running his own affairs without his mother's help, kindly though her ladyship's intentions were always meant.

At least Daniel proved himself very capable of finding his way to the spot Robina had suggested for the picnic without any trouble at all, for within what seemed a very short space of time he was drawing his curricle off the road, coming to a halt beneath the shading branches of a large yew.

Whilst Robina and the Dowager consulted on the exact spot to hold the picnic, Daniel organised the removal of the food baskets and rugs from the coach. The delicious aroma of roast chicken wafted through the air as the baskets were carried across the grass, making Sir Percy feel decidedly peckish, and he wasn't slow to voice the opinion that the contents of the baskets should be sampled before the champagne had chance to grow warm.

As no one objected to this, the Dowager ordered the servants to serve the food and drink immediately. Everyone, with the exception of Lord Phelps who ate sparingly, eagerly sampled each of the tempting offerings Cook had taken the trouble to prepare. Consequently, no one felt particularly energetic afterwards, and the game of cricket which Daniel had proposed earlier to keep his younger daughter entertained was postponed until the food had been given time to settle.

Hannah decided to follow Lord Phelps's example and sketch for a while. It was decided that the best view of the ruined priory could be obtained from a position close to the large wood which covered a substantial part of the landscape. A river meandered its way across the countryside close to the wood's edge, and nestling between a clump of trees on the far bank was what remained of the priory.

After spreading a blanket on the lush grass several yards from where Lord Phelps had chosen to position himself, Robina settled herself between the two girls. Hannah, a keen sketcher, was very quickly absorbed in the subject across the river, unlike her sister who swiftly lost interest, but who was persuaded to continue with her effort until she saw her father approaching.

Daniel paused to stare over Lord Phelps's shoulder, and was sufficiently impressed by what he saw to nod his head several times in approval, before he turned and moved slowly towards the girls.

'Phelps undeniably has talent,' he remarked in an undertone as he reached them.

He was generous in his praise of his elder daughter's effort too. He even managed to say something complimentary about Lizzie's rather hurried, halfhearted attempt, before finally coming to stand behind Robina.

'Well, now, what can one say about this effort, I wonder?' he remarked, after peering long and hard over her shoulder.

Robina, managing to school her features, continued with her drawing, just as though he were not there. Sketching had always been a favourite hobby of hers, an enjoyable way of passing those miserable, wet days when she could not venture out of doors. She had been told by many people, including her mother who was a severe critic when it came to judging the so-called female accomplishments, that she had undoubted talent. She knew her limitations, but was also very well aware that the subjects of her drawings were always instantly recognisable, and so was prepared to take any teasing in good part.

'That—er—object in the centre is the priory, I presume… Yes,' he muttered, turning his head on one side. 'If you look at it from this angle it does resemble a building…vaguely.'

'Oh, Papa! That is most unfair of you to make fun,' Hannah reproved. 'I wish I could sketch half so well as Robina.'

His brows rose. 'Robina?'

'Yes, well—but Robina gave me permission to call her by her first name.'

'And me too, Papa,' Lizzie informed him, abandoning her drawing completely now and scrambling to her feet. 'Did you know she has three sisters, and her papa gave them all boys' names, because he really wanted them to be boys?'

'No, he didn't, silly,' her elder sister corrected. 'He chose names for boys, and then changed them slightly when they all turned out to be girls.'

'He still wanted a boy. Robina said so,' Lizzie argued, before casting an enquiring glance up at her father. 'Did you want us to be boys, Papa?'

'No, sweetheart. I was more than happy with you and Hannah.'

This perfect response won him a bright smile from his younger offspring, as she caught hold of his hand. 'Come along, Papa. Let's go and explore the wood.'

'Very well, Lizzie, I'll come with you presently,' he responded, disengaging her hold. 'But first I must go and see if either your grandmama or Sir Percy wishes to accompany us. Don't you go off without me,' he warned, before striding back across the grass.

Lizzie, evidently not content to sit and await her father's return, decided to make use of a conveniently fallen tree to practise her balancing skills by walking back and forth along the length of the trunk, leaving Hannah and Robina in peace to continue with their sketching.

'I think that was very rude of Papa to say those unkind things about your picture,' Hannah remarked, once she knew her father was safely out of earshot. 'I never ever heard him criticise any of Mama's drawings. And yours is much better than any of hers that I ever saw.' She frowned suddenly. 'Mama didn't like it when people said unkind things about her pictures.'

Robina had gained the distinct impression already from odd remarks the girls had made that both of them remembered their lovely mother with deep affection, most especially Hannah who, being the elder by some three years, recalled things about their mother rather better than Lizzie did. Both had coped remarkably well with their sad loss, and both were touchingly close to their father.

Robina didn't suppose for a moment that Hannah's last remark had been intended as a slur on her mother's character. Evidently, though, the late Lady Exmouth either did not appreciate criticism, or objected most strongly to being teased. Robina had grown accustomed to both throughout her life, and so had not taken his lordship's less than flattering remarks to heart.

'Your papa, I've discovered, is a great tease. He certainly enjoys tormenting me from time to time.'

'He certainly teases Lizzie and me.' Hannah's frown returned. 'I cannot recall his ever teasing Mama, though.'

She looked across at Lord Phelps, who had remained quietly absorbed in what he was doing since he had selected his spot on the grass. 'He's very handsome, isn't he?'

'Very,' Robina agreed, thinking that girls grew up rather quickly these days. She could not recall ever noticing whether a gentleman was handsome or not when she had been Hannah's age. She could, however, remember wandering off by herself, when she had been specifically requested not to do so, just as Lizzie, the little monkey, appeared to have done.

'Your sister hasn't bothered to await your father's return, I see,' she said, placing her sketch pad carefully to one side, before rising to her feet in one graceful movement. 'I had better go and check she isn't getting into mischief.'

'She's always doing that,' Hannah grumbled. 'I had better come with you. One of these days she's going to get herself lost. Then she'll be sorry!'

As they entered the wood, they could see no sign of the girl. Experienced in the ways of her sister, Hannah voiced her suspicion that Lizzie had possibly gone down to the river. 'She would do that, as Papa particularly requested her not to do so.'

Robina could not forbear a smile. She could fully appreciate the girl's chagrin. Having three younger sisters, she knew well enough how annoying they could be on occasions, but she had never been tempted to play the talebearer, and she doubted that Hannah would ever consider doing so either.

'In that case we'd better search there first,' Robina suggested, leading the way through the undergrowth.

The long grass and bracken brushed against her skirts, but there was little she could do to protect them from the inevitable staining. Besides which, she was more concerned about Lizzie than her own appearance.

They arrived at the riverbank without catching a glimpse of the truant, but thankfully after a few moments Robina detected a gleeful chuckle in response to Hannah's calling. 'She's further along the bank,' she said, swiftly locating the direction of the faint noise.

Keeping a safe distance from the edge of the slippery, sloping bank, they continued to forge a path through the thick undergrowth, and eventually spotted the girl, clinging monkey-fashion to the overhanging branch of a tree which leaned some way out across the river.

'Come back at once, Lizzie!' Hannah ordered, a clear note of alarm in her voice, which Robina could quite understand. The branch was swaying precariously under Lizzie's weight. 'Come back at once, do you hear, or I'll go and fetch Papa!'

'Oh, very well,' Lizzie responded, evidently having taken her sister's threat seriously, and was just beginning to edge her way slowly back when there was the unmistakable sound of splintering wood. Hannah let out a scream as Lizzie, immediately losing her grasp, dropped into the water, quickly disappearing into the murky depths.

Refusing to panic, Robina quickly dispatched Hannah to collect her father. Lizzie had landed in the water several yards from the bank, too far out to reach with a substantial stick, so Robina did not waste precious time in trying to make the attempt and swiftly removed both bonnet and shoes.

Only that morning she had been entertaining Exmouth's daughters with amusing tales of her own childhood exploits, some of which she was forced to admit she was now less than proud. However, one secret pastime in which she had never regretted indulging was learning to swim.

Her good friend Lady Sophia Cleeve had been taught to do so by her elder brother Lord Angmering, and had been eager to share this rare female accomplishment with her good friend the vicar's daughter. The lake on the vast Cleeve estate had been an ideal place to learn, and Robina, after a tentative beginning, had soon lost her fear of the water and had surprisingly excelled at this outdoor pursuit. Never had she been more grateful for this natural ability than now, for the instant she dived into the water her worst fears were confirmed.

The river looked peaceful, gently flowing, but beneath the surface were hidden currents and, worse still, beds of tangled reeds, just waiting to entwine themselves round an ankle or leg and slowly draw some poor unsuspecting soul slowly downwards to his death. Robina could feel those perilous green tendrils flicking against her skirts as she began to tread water, frantically searching for a sign of the little girl who moments before had been gasping and spluttering above the water line, but who now was nowhere to be seen. Then, blessedly, she noticed a stream of bubbles rising just a few yards away, and detected a flash of blue just beneath the surface.

She reached the exact spot in seconds. The water was murky, heavily silted, and visibility was poor, but thankfully after one swift plunge beneath the surface she made contact with the girl and, holding fast to the sleeve of the bright blue dress, she brought Lizzie to the surface.

Coughing, spluttering and understandably terrified, Lizzie entwined her little arms vicelike about Robina's neck, almost sending them both plunging into the murky depths once more. Somehow Robina managed to disengage those frantically clutching arms and manoeuvre the petrified girl into a position whereby she could manage to get them both safely back to the bank.

Fighting the current, and Lizzie's continuing frantic struggles, Robina was almost spent by the time she reached her goal. Even at the river's edge the water was too deep for her to stand, and the bank too steep for her to climb, even if she had possessed sufficient strength to make the attempt. The only thing she could do was hold fast with her free hand to one of the gnarled tree roots protruding from the earth, and pray that help was not slow in coming.

Thankfully her prayers were answered. Just when she thought she could hold neither Lizzie nor her lifeline a moment longer, a deeply reassuring voice sounded from just above and a strong masculine hand reached down to relieve her of the heavy burden she had successfully saved from a watery grave.

The next moment her own wrists were encircled by long, masculine fingers and she was blessedly raised from the water herself, and held fast to a stone hard chest. She clung to her rescuer, entwining her arms about the strong column of his neck in much the same way as Lizzie had done to her only minutes before. Her deliverer did not appear to object in the least, for he made not the least attempt to remove them as he murmured words of comfort, none of which she could clearly hear above the pounding in her temples and her valiant efforts to regain her breath.

Only when her breathing became more regular, and she felt she could stand without assistance, did she disengage herself from the gentle hold in time to witness the Dowager arrive on the scene, carrying a blanket, and Sir Percy, breathing harder than she was now doing herself, bringing up the rear.

The Dowager, wasting not a moment in wrapping the frightened and sobbing Lizzie in the woollen rug, glanced across in Robina's direction and let out an exclamation of dismay.

'By Jove!' Sir Percy muttered, following the direction of her gaze, and promptly felt for his quizzing-glass.

'Daniel, your coat...quickly,' her ladyship ordered in rapidly fading accents. 'The poor child must be freezing.'

After one brief glance in Robina's direction, Daniel could appreciate fully his mother's concern, and quite understand too why Sir Percy's gaze betrayed an earthy masculine appreciation.

Robina's wet gown clung to her like a second skin, leaving absolutely nothing to the imagination.

Quickly suppressing his own strong desire to look his fill, and sublimely ignoring Robina's half-hearted attempt not to accept the garment, he slipped the jacket about her shoulders, and then wasted no further time in getting the perpetrator of what might well have turned out to be a tragic incident back to the coach.

Scooping Lizzie up in his arms, he led the way out of the wood, leaving Robina to the tender care of his mother. By the time they had arrived at the edge of the wood, Robina had managed to assure the Dowager that, apart from a slightly bruised and grazed right hand, and the fact that she was now feeling a little chilled, she was none the worse for her ordeal.

'Well, at least we can do something about making you a little warmer,' Sir Percy announced, and went striding across the grass towards Lord Phelps.

'Miss Perceval has a greater need of this than you, sir!' he snapped, a distinct note of impatience in his voice, and did no more than literally tug the rug from beneath the startled young Earl, almost sending him toppling over on to the grass.

'Good heavens!' he remarked, turning startled eyes towards Robina.

For someone who appeared to be living in another world most of the time, his gaze on occasions could be most disconcerting, and remarkably acute, noting the smallest detail. 'Has there been an accident?' he asked, thereby betraying the fact that he hadn't taken the faintest interest in anything going on about him since the moment he had positioned himself on the grass. 'Did you fall into the river, Miss Perceval?'

Sir Percy clapped a hand over his eyes. 'Heaven spare us!' he muttered and, without attempting a further explanation, escorted the highly amused ladies back to the coach.

Later, after being stripped of her sodden, mud-stained garments, Robina eased her aching limbs in a bath of warm scented water. Pinner, who had always betrayed a great fondness for her, fussed about like a mother hen, nothing being too much trouble. Robina accepted this exaggerated cosseting with a good grace, but when Pinner, having helped the heroine of the day to restore her normally faultless appearance, announced that the doctor had been asked to call and would undoubtedly be paying a visit to the room very shortly,

Robina decided that she had received more than enough attention for one day.

'I have no wish to see any doctor, Pinner. Besides, except for a sore hand, there's nothing whatsoever the matter with me, and I've absolutely no intention of wasting the doctor's valuable time over such a trivial matter.'

'The master insisted, miss.'

For the first time ever Pinner saw the light of battle flash in a pair of blue eyes, but whatever the normally even-tempered vicar's daughter might have been about to retort was held in check, for the door opened and a round little man, carrying a leather bag, entered the room.

Smiling like some indulgent uncle, the doctor listened patiently to all Robina's assurances that she was perfectly well, and then promptly set about his work, declaring when he had finished the brief examination that she was in excellent health, and that he would send his man round with a jar of salve for the injured hand.

'Have you had chance to examine Miss Courtney, Doctor?'

'Yes, ma'am. She's none the worse for her ordeal.' He tutted. 'Always been an excitable child, of course. Just like her dear mama—highly strung. I've left something to help her sleep tonight, and

I shall call again in the morning, but I do not envisage any complications arising from the day's unfortunate escapade.'

'His lordship was very cross with her,' Pinner divulged when the doctor had left the room. 'Administered a proper scold, so I've been told. Said she had to stay in bed for the rest of the day, and if she dared to defy him, he'd pack her straight back to Courtney Place.'

'Oh dear,' Robina muttered, feeling a little sorry for the girl, but Pinner was of a different mind.

'If you ask me, she's been allowed to get away with things for far too long, miss. I'm not saying that one oughtn't to have made allowances after her mother died, but Miss Lizzie's always had a tendency to be naughty. I think the master now realises he must start to take a firmer hand with her before she becomes thoroughly spoilt. Why, I overheard his lordship telling the mistress that if you hadn't been there to save Miss Lizzie, it would have been too late by the time he'd reached the river.' There was a suspicion of tears in the maid's eyes. 'A real heroine you be, miss.'

Feeling acutely embarrassed by this unmerited praise, Robina did her best to try to assure the maid that she wasn't in the least brave, and that she had done no more than most other people would have done in similar circumstances, but Pinner would accept none of it. As far as she was concerned the vicar's daughter was one of those rare beings touched by God: someone special, someone to be revered, and nothing Robina could say would detract her from this belief.

So, deciding the best course was to allow the passage of time to restore the maid's sound common sense, Robina took herself off to the girls' room to check on Lizzie's progress for herself. She was not unduly worried about the child. The girl, quite naturally, had been very frightened by the ordeal, and her subdued state throughout the entire carriage journey back to the house had been understandable in the circumstances. Robina didn't suppose for a moment that Lizzie was in the least danger of succumbing to this unusual lethargy for any great length of time, and was not in the least surprised to discover her sitting up in bed, quite happily listening to her elder sister reading a story.

Her arrival certainly gave rise to mixed reactions: Hannah, rising from the chair placed by the bed, and smiling brightly, was obviously delighted to see her; Lizzie, after one very guilty glance across the room, lowered her eyes, suddenly finding the bedcovers of immense interest.

Being vastly experienced in the ways of young

girls, Robina understood the reason behind this distinct lack of enthusiasm on the part of the younger sister. 'I haven't come here with the intention of scolding.'

The assurance won an instant response: a decidedly mischievous smile, swiftly followed by a wicked chuckle. 'Wasn't it exciting, Robina! A real adventure we've had today!'

'Exciting…?' Hannah glanced at her sister in dismay. 'You might have died, you silly little idiot! You know what Papa said—if Robina hadn't been there to save you, you wouldn't be here now.'

'Well, yes…I know that,' Lizzie reluctantly conceded. 'But she was there, so it was all right, wasn't it?'

Hannah, much to Robina's intense amusement, raised her hands ceilingwards in a despairing gesture. 'I give up! You're hopeless…completely hopeless. You know what Papa told you would happen if you ever disobeyed him again,' she reminded her. 'And he means it. He was very cross.'

'I know,' Lizzie mumbled, absently plucking at the bed covers. 'And I've promised him I won't. I shan't go near a river again until he's taught us how to swim.' She raised excited eyes to Robina, as her rescuer came forward to stand by the bed.

'Papa has said that he's going to teach both Hannah and me how to swim when he returns home in the autumn. Was it your papa who taught you how to swim?'

'Er—not exactly, no,' she admitted, wondering how her father would react if he was ever to discover his eldest daughter's unusual accomplishment. She doubted very much that he would display quite the enthusiasm which Lord Exmouth was betraying for his own daughters to learn how to swim. 'No, it was a friend of mine who taught me.'

'Papa says that girls ought to learn as well as boys, and he cannot think why he never thought of teaching us before,' Hannah divulged, appearing less enthusiastic than her younger sister at the prospect of taking to the water. 'I shouldn't mind learning if…well, if you were to teach me, Robina,' she admitted at last, colouring slightly. 'After all, it isn't very seemly, is it?'

'Don't be silly!' Lizzie scoffed, when Robina, quite understanding the older girl's modesty, was about to suggest that, if she could swim, perhaps Miss Halliwell might be persuaded to offer instruction. 'After all, Papa didn't take any notice at all of Robina when he pulled her from the river,' Lizzie continued, blithely ignoring her sister's swift warning glance. 'And she looked as if she wasn't wearing any clothes at all.'

'Lizzie, how could you!' Hannah reproved, but the damage was already done. Poor Robina's face had turned a bright red, for she knew the girl had spoken no less than the truth.

She had noticed herself the look of blatant admiration on Sir Percy's face, but at the time had thought that perhaps he had been much impressed by her act of bravery in rescuing Daniel's daughter from the murky depths of the river. How foolish she had been! She ought to have realised that her thin muslin gown, though modestly styled and perfectly respectable for a young lady to wear, would become virtually transparent when wet.

She remembered something else too: the way Daniel had clasped her to him; the way she had clung to him in return, experiencing in those few moments a wonderful feeling of being protected, cherished. Had he merely held her that way in order to conceal her less than modest state? The thought that this might indeed have been the case was, strangely, considerably more daunting than discovering that she had quite innocently been displaying her charms to appreciative masculine eyes.

Suddenly aware that two pairs of young eyes were regarding her now, she tried to make light of the matter, and then quickly changed the subject by suggesting things they could do together whilst the girls remained in Brighton. She might well have succeeded in thrusting the memory of that embarrassing incident from her mind completely had she not a few minutes later, when she had left the room, come face to face with Daniel mounting the stairs.

There was absolutely no way of avoiding the encounter. To have turned and run back up the staircase to the sanctuary of her own room would, she didn't doubt for a moment, have given rise to the most appalling conjecture on Daniel's part. Much better to face him now, she decided, and try to make light of the day's escapade.

'I have just popped in to see how that little mermaid of yours goes on. I do not think she is any the worse for her ordeal.'

'And you?' he asked gently, coming to a halt two steps below, and staring up at a sweet face that betrayed becoming rosy tints of embarrassment.

'Oh, I'm fine. We Northamptonshire girls come from good earthy stock, you know,' she said airily. 'We're remarkably robust.'

'Remarkably brave too,' he responded softly. He reached for her right hand, noticing it trembling

Chapter Seven

Robina would never have supposed for a moment that any action of hers would result in such recognition. The servants, she quickly discovered, simply couldn't do enough for her, treating her with a kind of reverence whenever she emerged from the bed-chamber. She noticed that more of her favourite dishes appeared on the menu, and was repeatedly informed by both Stebbings and Pinner that Cook was more than willing to prepare any other little delicacies that Miss Perceval might be wishful to sample.

Unfortunately this unexpected attention was not limited to members of the household. An account of the incident by the river, possibly divulged initially by Sir Percy Lovell, quickly spread throughout Brighton society, and not a day went by without the house being invaded by a stream of inquisitive visitors, determined to discover for themselves if there was any truth in the story circulating about Miss Robina Perceval's courageous act.

Vases of beautiful flowers began to appear in every room in the house, including a huge arrangement of highly scented white lilies, sent by Lord Phelps and his mother. Daniel's brow was seen to darken considerably each time he passed by them in the hall, though whether it was the powerful scent of which he disapproved, or from whence they came, no one was very sure.

Robina comforted herself in the knowledge that shallow society would find a new source of interest given time, and that she would not forever remain an object of attention wherever she went. Thankfully, there had been a noticeable reduction of interest displayed when the day arrived for Hannah and Lizzie to leave Brighton and continue their journey to Dorset.

Robina was sorry to see them go, for she had become genuinely attached to the sisters, but she was happy to think that their departure would herald their father's return to the house. No matter how enjoyable she had found the girls' company, she couldn't deny that she had missed very much those times she and Daniel had spent together, happily reading in companionable silence, or playing cards.

Sadly he betrayed no signs of desiring an immediate return to the house, and appeared more than content to remain for the time being at least with his good friend Montague Merrell. Strangely enough the Dowager did not appear particularly concerned over her son's seeming reluctance to take up residence with them again. In fact, she appeared too excited by their invitation to dine at the Pavilion to concern herself with much else.

The Regent's arrival in Brighton brought a further influx of visitors to the town, and a noticeable increase in social events. Not an evening passed without Robina spending an hour or so in her bedchamber, preparing to attend some party or other, and on the day they were due to dine at the Pavilion, Pinner took longer than ever to dress Robina's hair and to fasten her into the lovely kingfisher-blue silk gown which she had donned only once before, when she had worn it on the occasion of her good friend Lady Sophia Cleeve's engagement party.

Daniel had kindly consented to escort them, and kept Robina in a high state of amusement throughout the short carriage journey by passing rather disparaging remarks concerning the Regent's garish taste in décor, and the deplorable alterations His Royal Highness continued to make to his 'little retreat' by the sea.

Robina, although excited at the prospect of dining at the Pavilion, could not but agree with Daniel's opinions. Each room she passed through in the famous building was richly decorated and sumptuously furnished, no expense having been spared. The choice of décor, however, certainly wouldn't have been to everyone's taste, and most certainly wasn't to her own. Simplicity and sobriety were not words in the Regent's vocabulary it seemed. There was evidence of his extravagance everywhere, most especially in the dining-room, where an amazing number of richly dressed dishes were placed on the table.

As the evening wore on, and many, many more guests began to arrive, the atmosphere in the Saloon, where dancing was being held, became increasingly oppressive. Robina managed to locate a slightly cooler spot in one corner, and attempted to conceal herself behind the gracefully spreading foliage of a conveniently positioned potted palm, while she studied the dancers, all dressed in their finest, their clothes and bodies glimmering with precious jewels.

Unfortunately, as had happened more frequently of late, her mind began to dwell on what the future might hold in store for her once she had left all the delights of Brighton behind her, and she quite failed to notice a certain tall, athletic figure quietly approaching.

'And what's all this?' The familiar, attractive voice made her start. 'It isn't like you, my little bird, to skulk away in a corner.'

'I was not skulking, as you call it,' she responded, wondering if he had been watching her for some little time, 'merely trying to make myself as inconspicuous as possible. It's so very warm in here, Daniel. I wouldn't dare risk a further period on the dance-floor, and was doing my level best to avoid being asked.'

He appeared to accept this explanation readily enough. 'Yes, it's certainly oppressive. Would you care for a stroll in the conservatory? You might find it a little less uncomfortable out there.'

She didn't need to think twice about it, and linked her arm through his, willingly accepting his escort into the huge glass construction which was noticeably cooler and far less congested, though there were more than one or two couples lurking amidst the greenery.

'What were you thinking about, Robin?' he

asked, after they had strolled to the end and seated themselves in two of the wicker chairs. 'You appeared to be in a world of your own. Aren't you enjoying these opulent royal surroundings?'

'Very much, though I do find them a little overwhelming.'

The answer came swiftly enough, but to one who had made an intense study of her moods, Daniel found the reply just a little too mechanical, as though part of her mind remained elsewhere. 'Is something troubling you, Robin?' he asked gently, but she made no attempt to respond this time. 'Come, child, we are friends, are we not? True friends should never be afraid to confide in each other.'

Friends...? Once she had found it such a comfort to think of him in that light, but now... 'I was thinking of how very much I've enjoyed my time here in Brighton. Surprisingly enough, much more so than I did my weeks in the capital.'

He appeared decidedly sceptical. 'You'll forgive me for saying so, Robin, but you looked anything but contented a few minutes ago.'

She couldn't help but smile at the swiftness and honesty of his response. 'If that is so then it was the thought of having to leave all this behind when I return to Abbot Quincey.' She discovered she was equally powerless to prevent a sigh escaping. 'I'm becoming far too contented with this kind of life, Daniel. It is quite worrying.'

He regarded her in silence, his expression quite unreadable now. 'What convinces you that you must abandon this kind of life? If you do not relish the prospect of returning to Northamptonshire, there must surely be other options open to you.'

'Such as what?'

'Marriage.' There was more than just a hint of cynicism in the smile he cast her. 'After all, it was with the intention of finding yourself a husband that you left Abbot Quincey in the first place.'

She wasn't in the least offended by this. Daniel would never be deliberately hurtful, but at the same time he was never afraid to speak his mind, and she had grown quite accustomed to the occasional blunt remark.

'You make it sound so very mercenary,' she responded, not attempting to deny it. 'Which, of course, it is. Most young women who embark on a London Season do so with that very goal in mind. And I was, I suppose, luckier than most,' she continued, after a moment's reflection. 'I did at least receive two proposals of marriage, neither of which I regretted refusing.'

She decided not to add that this was done with

her mother's full approval, and in the hope that a third and far more advantageous offer might be forthcoming from Daniel himself. 'Both gentlemen were very respectable, but my feelings were not engaged.'

Once again she found herself on the receiving end of one of those penetrating brown-eyed stares. 'And has no suitable gentleman succeeded in capturing your interest since your arrival in Brighton? Mr Frederick Ainsley, for instance? He has been increasingly attentive in recent weeks, and you do not appear averse to his company.'

She certainly wasn't averse to the gentlemanly Mr Ainsley's company. She liked him very well, had done so from their very first meeting. Whether she would be content to spend the rest of her life with him was quite another matter entirely.

Strangely enough, Robina had never once seriously considered the possibility of a union with Frederick Ainsley. She didn't doubt for a moment that he would make both a considerate and loving husband. In many ways he reminded her of her own father. Both were intelligent and both were sincerely dedicated to their chosen profession. Therein, she supposed, lay the reason why she had no intention of allowing her relationship with Mr Ainsley to deepen.

She had never made any secret of the fact that she had enjoyed a very happy childhood in Abbot Quincey. None the less, she experienced no desire whatsoever to exchange life in one vicarage for life in another.

She had now grown accustomed to a completely different lifestyle. And she loved it! It wasn't that she wished for a future that was just one long round of socialising and parties. Oh, no, that would not appeal to her in the least! She wanted marriage and children. But most important of all she wished to marry a man whom she could love and respect. Her perfect mate was out there somewhere, she felt certain of it, and yet his image continued to elude her, remaining just a blur in her mind's eye.

'Yes, I should like to marry, Daniel. But, if and when I do, it will be to a man I love,' she admitted at last, thereby betraying her inmost thoughts. 'I would never marry just for security, or just to have a home of my own.'

There was a discernible note of self-consciousness in her little trill of laughter. 'Oh, I don't know, Daniel. Perhaps I expect too much from life. I've been luckier than most, I know. It's just that… How can I explain it?…I suppose it's just that nothing very exciting has ever happened to me. Every girl dreams of meeting her knight in shining armour, a brave Sir Galahad who will rescue her from danger, and then fall hopelessly in love with her.

'Yes, well, may you laugh,' she went on when a rich masculine rumble greeted this confession. 'You're a man. No doubt you've enjoyed a deal of excitement in your life; whereas mine, up until a few weeks ago, has been singularly uneventful.'

Daniel's smile remained, but there was no mistaking the sincerity in his voice as he said, 'Yes, I rather fancy I do understand, my little bird. A little excitement from time to time does no one any harm. So, you're hoping to meet your Sir Lancelot.'

'Galahad,' she corrected, feeling extremely foolish now at having confessed to a rather childish fancy. 'But as that is unlikely ever to happen, I'm desperately striving to resign myself to life as a governess.'

'Dear me,' he murmured. 'That's a comedown from a life with a brave knight.'

'True,' she agreed, 'but possibly more realistic.'

Easily removing the fan from her clasp, Daniel opened it to its fullest extent to study the decoration of delicately painted flowers. 'Have you forgotten Mama's suggestion that you might like to consider becoming her permanent companion?'

Robina clearly recalled the subject being raised, but hadn't taken her ladyship's remarks seriously. 'She was jesting, surely?'

'No, I do not believe so, child. She's extremely fond of you.'

He looked as if he was about to say something further, but then evidently thought better of it, and promptly handed back her fan before rising to his feet. 'There will be time enough for you to consider my mother's proposal. The Brighton Season is far from over, so let us return to the Saloon now and continue to enjoy it.'

They were halfway down the huge glass construction when they noticed a number of persons beginning to gather near the door. The little group suddenly parted, and into the conservatory strolled Daniel's very good friend Montague Merrell, accompanied by none other than the Regent himself.

Robina knew, of course, that Mr Merrell was a close friend of the future king. She had seen Mr Merrell, together with several others, enter the room with the Regent shortly before it was time to go in to dinner. There had been no opportunity of being introduced to the Regent then; there was no chance of avoiding it now. His Royal Highness took one glance down the conservatory and his plump features creased in a smile of instant recognition.

'Exmouth, old fellow!' He came forward, moving with surprising grace for a gentleman of his ample proportions. 'Monty here informed me that you were amongst the guests tonight. How good it is to see you in society once more!'

'Thank you, sir.' Daniel noticed the future monarch's eyes stray in Robina's direction, and hurriedly presented her before the totally wrong conclusion could be drawn.

Robina, executing a graceful curtsey, discovered her hand captured in warm, podgy fingers. 'Delightful! Delightful!' beamed the Regent, eyeing her approvingly, and making her feel like a particularly tasty morsel presented to him on a plate.

'Miss Perceval is at present residing with us in Brighton, sir… And is here under my mother's protection,' Daniel added, just in case the Regent should still be harbouring any doubts as to Robina's respectability.

'Excellent!' The future king, after one last squeeze of the slender fingers, released his hold on Robina's hand. 'And how is your dear mother, Exmouth? In good health, I trust?'

'In fine fettle, sir, as always.'

'Excellent, excellent!' he said again, before

turning to Merrell. 'Well, Monty, let us leave Exmouth to escort this delightful young lady to the safety of his mother's side, and go and find Wilmington. You said he was also here tonight, I seem to remember.'

'Indeed he is,' Mr Merrell responded and, after casting a sly wink in Daniel's direction, accompanied the Regent back to the Saloon.

Daniel and Robina followed at a discreet distance, and eventually found the Dowager amidst a small group at the far end of the room.

'I have been ordered by no less a personage than the Regent himself to restore Robina to your protection,' Daniel divulged, after extricating his mother from the small group. 'And as I wouldn't dare to disobey a royal command, here she is.'

'Where on earth have you been, child? The last time I saw you, you were dancing with Lord Farley.'

'Oh, she has gone up in the world since then, Mama,' Daniel put in before Robina could even attempt to offer an explanation for her long absence. 'She has been hobnobbing with royalty.'

'Truly?' The Dowager's excited glance darted between the two. 'You've met the Regent, child? Did you introduce her, Daniel? I was hoping to present you. What did you think of our future king?'

'Rather overwhelming, ma'am.'

'Rather overweight, you mean,' the Dowager corrected.

'Careful, Mama,' her son warned. 'There are those who have been banished for saying less.'

Lady Exmouth was about to say that she had spoken no less than the truth, when an undignified squeal reached her ears, and she turned to discover a vivacious damsel, dressed in an amber-coloured gown, bearing down upon them.

'Heavens above!' she exclaimed, wrapping her arms about the perpetrator of the unladylike squeal. 'What on earth are you doing here, child?'

'The same as you, I should imagine, Aunt Lavinia.'

Disengaging herself from the loving embrace, the new arrival turned to Daniel and unashamedly placed a smacking kiss on his cheek. 'Never expected to bump in to you here, my dear cousin,' she admitted, staring up at him with more than just a hint of devilment in her dark eyes. 'Always thought you had more taste. My, my, how you have changed!'

'Which you patently have not, you outrageous baggage!' he retorted, smiling down into twinkling brown eyes. 'Now, behave yourself for a moment, and allow me to present Miss Robina Perceval to you...Robin,' he added turning to her, 'this is my cousin, Lady Arabella Tolliver, the scourge of my life.'

'Horrid creature!' Laughing, Lady Tolliver reached for Robina's hand, and held it fast in both her own. 'How very pleased I am to make your acquaintance, Miss Perceval. I had heard rumours that dear Aunt Lavinia had taken a pretty girl under her protective wing.'

'And before you are tempted into further indiscretion,' her ladyship put in hurriedly, 'I think we had better find ourselves some quiet corner, preferably somewhere where we are able to sit down.'

She turned to her son in time to catch the amused glint in his eyes, and hurriedly asked if he would be kind enough to fetch them refreshments. Then without further ado, she ushered the young ladies to the farthest corner of the room, where she was lucky enough to find three vacant chairs.

'Now, Arabella,' she began, when they had all seated themselves. 'What brings you to Brighton? You never mentioned you were planning a visit in your last letter.'

'Good gracious, Aunt Lavinia! You ought to know me better than that by now. I never make plans. I do everything on the spur of the moment. Besides, why shouldn't I be here? My period of mourning was over weeks ago.' She cast a rather wistful glance down at the skirts of her fetching amber-coloured gown. 'Pity really…I looked quite becoming in widow's weeds.'

'Arabella, really!' her aunt reproved, striving not to laugh. 'What are people to think when you talk that way!'

She then turned to Robina, who was also doing her level best not to laugh at the lively Lady Tolliver's remarks. 'If you have not already guessed, my dear, this outrageous young woman is my niece, the only daughter of my dear departed sister Emily. Sadly my sister died giving birth to a stillborn child, and my niece spent long periods during her childhood with us at Courtney Place. I believe she looked upon the house as her second home, and Daniel as her brother.'

'I certainly looked upon the Place as home, Aunt, but whether I ever thought of Daniel as my brother is quite another matter.'

Robina certainly detected the wry edge in Lady Tolliver's voice. Whether the Dowager did or not was difficult to judge, for her attention was diverted in the next moment by her son's approach, bringing with him a footman, bearing four glasses of champagne on a silver tray. Once they had all sampled their refreshments, Daniel turned to his cousin, asking where she was staying.

'Dear Roderick rented a house for the duration of the summer. The poor dear would not hear of leaving me behind when I contracted a troublesome cold, which I simply could not shake off. We planned to arrive in the middle of June, but only succeeded in leaving Devonshire a few days ago.'

'And you are fully restored to health now, I trust?'

'Yes, Cousin, and eager to make up for all the time we've lost.' Her rather wide mouth curled into a sudden smile. 'Oh, there's dear Roddy now,' she announced, glancing in the direction of the main door. 'Do go over and rescue him from Lord Crawford, Daniel. I do not wish for him to be persuaded into indulging in a game of chance with that inveterate gambler. Roddy's no card player, and I should hate to discover in the morning that he's lost the entire family fortune.'

She laughed as her cousin moved away to do her bidding. 'It is so amusing having a stepson virtually the same age as oneself. Most people seeing us together automatically assume that we're husband and wife.'

Robina, having followed his progress across the room, saw Daniel shake the hand of a sandy-haired gentleman of medium height, and thought it highly likely that most people who were not acquainted with them would possibly think that Lady Tolliver and Sir Roderick were married. She was intrigued to learn more about Daniel's spirited cousin, but was destined to discover nothing further that evening, for they were joined by several of the Dowager's particular friends, and Lady Tolliver soon afterwards drifted away to mix with the other guests.

Robina caught sight of her again on only three occasions throughout the remainder of the evening. Each time she was clinging possessively to Daniel's arm. He appeared not in the least displeased at being monopolised by her. In fact, he looked far happier than Robina had ever seen him look before. It ought, she knew, to have given her a great deal of pleasure to think that Daniel was blissfully contented in his cousin's company, but it did not. Perversely it had the opposite effect, and she left the Pavilion later that night feeling decidedly dispirited.

Chapter Eight

The following morning Robina received a letter from her family, confirming the surprising notice she had read in the newspaper two weeks before, announcing her cousin Hester's betrothal to Lord Dungarran.

She shook her head, still finding it difficult to believe. 'Well, apparently it is true,' she declared to Lady Exmouth, who sat opposite her at the breakfast table, happily nibbling her way through a second delicious buttered roll. 'Yet I'm still finding it hard to believe. Hester never displayed the least interest in finding herself a husband. Her first Season was a complete disaster. It put her off the idea of matrimony altogether.'

'No, not entirely, my dear,' Lady Exmouth corrected. 'Evidently Lord Dungarran persuaded her to change her mind, though I must say I cannot recall your cousin betraying much interest in any gentleman on the occasions I saw her in London. But, then, some young ladies are more adept at concealing their feelings than others, are they not?'

After debating for a moment, she weakened and reached for a third buttered roll. 'Does your mother reveal any other details in her letter?'

Robina scanned the single sheet written in her mother's beautifully flowing hand. 'Only that the engagement was announced on the day of the fête. What a pity I wasn't there to celebrate with the family! Uncle James and Aunt Eleanor must be absolutely delighted.'

She shook her head, smiling to herself as a thought suddenly occurred to her. 'Do you know, ma'am, before we, Lady Sophia Cleeve, Hester and myself, that is, left Northamptonshire all those weeks ago, I never imagined that I would be the only one amongst us who would return home not betrothed. In fact, if I'm honest, I would be forced to admit that I considered it more than likely that I would be the only one to find herself engaged at the end of the Season.'

The hand raising the Dowager's coffee-cup to her lips checked for a moment. 'There's still plenty of time for you to become so, my dear. After all, you are not scheduled to return home until the autumn.'

'That is precisely what Daniel himself said,' Robina responded before she quite realised what she was disclosing, and noticed the sudden alert expression flicker over her interested companion's features.

That relaxed and easy-going manner of the Dowager's was extremely deceptive. It might lead one to suppose that she happily existed in a world of her own for the most part, content to let the more mundane day to day events pass her by; whereas, in fact, very little escaped her notice.

'Yes—er—well, as I mentioned to him last night,' she hurriedly continued, 'I would never marry simply for security and to acquire a home of my own.'

'Did you really say that to my son?' Lady Exmouth appeared genuinely impressed. 'Good for you, child!'

Robina stared across the breakfast table, puzzled by this surprising reaction to her disclosure. Surely, if Lady Exmouth continued to retain the hope of a marriage between her son and the Vicar of Abbot Quincey's daughter, she ought not to be happy to learn that the girl whom she considered highly suitable for a future daughter-in-law could not be persuaded to marry for either wealth or rank? Perhaps the Dowager had undergone a change of heart since her arrival in Brighton, and had come to the conclusion that her son and the vicar's daughter simply wouldn't suit, Robina mused, unexpectedly experiencing a feeling of bitter disappointment, and quickly changed the subject by enquiring if they could expect a visit from Lady Tolliver.

'Good gracious, child! I would never attempt to predict what that madcap niece of mine plans to do. She's a law unto herself!'

Disappointment was swiftly replaced by a strong feeling of resentment, as an image of Lady Tolliver, clinging like a limpet to Daniel's arm the previous evening, suddenly appeared before Robina's mind's eye.

'Daniel gave me the distinct impression that he is very fond of his cousin, ma'am,' she remarked in a casual tone, while desperately striving to control the wealth of strange sensations welling up inside. 'They are—er—more like brother and sister, didn't you say?'

'They always seemed so to me, and yet... Oh, I don't know, dear.' Her ladyship's lips curled into a reminiscent smile. 'I suppose at one time I imagined they might make a match of it. Arabella has no looks to speak of, but she has many other wonderful qualities to compensate for lack of beauty. She's intelligent and witty, and so full of life.' She shook her head, her smile quickly fading. 'I'm afraid, though, she could never compete with Clarissa, at least not in looks... Very few females ever could.'

Learning this ought to have improved Robina's state of mind; perversely, it did not. For some obscure reason she seemed incapable of controlling that unwholesome feeling of resentment. If anything it was increasing to encompass both Lady Tolliver and the late Lady Exmouth.

'Strangely enough Arabella was one of the very few people who thought Daniel was making a mistake in marrying Clarissa,' Lady Exmouth divulged, thereby instantly regaining Robina's full attention. 'And I do not believe her opinion was fuelled by jealousy. She genuinely seemed to feel that they would not suit. Of course there were others, like my good friend Sir Percy, who voiced their feelings of unease too, but their objections in the main stemmed from the fact that they considered Daniel too young for marriage.'

'What were your niece's objections, ma'am?' Robina prompted when the Dowager, with a far-away look in her eyes, fell silent once more. 'Did she ever offer an explanation for her disapproval?'

'No, I do not recall that she ever did, my dear. She and Clarissa played together a great deal when children, so Arabella knew her very well.' She shrugged. 'Perhaps my niece perceived something in Clarissa's nature that she didn't quite like. After all, no one is perfect. We all have our faults, little idiosyncrasies that others find irritating.'

This was certainly true. Robina had always been very close to her sisters, and loved them all dearly, but that didn't mean that she was blind to their faults, or did not find them quite annoying on occasions.

It would have been interesting to discover precisely what flaw Arabella had perceived in the late Lady Exmouth's nature, but as the Dowager evidently didn't know, there was little point in pursuing the subject, so Robina changed the conversation once again by remarking, 'From what Lady Tolliver was saying last night, I gained the distinct impression that her husband was a good deal older than herself.'

'Yes, dear, he was. It must be a trait with the females in my family to prefer older men. As I believe I've mentioned before, Daniel's dear papa was a good deal older than myself. Arabella's papa was much older than my sister, and Arabella herself married a gentleman old enough to be her own father.' Smiling, she shook her head. 'I must confess that I was surprised when my niece agreed to accept Sir Henry's proposal. She was always such a lively girl, never still for a moment, and I suppose I expected her to choose some dashing young blade. But no, she chose the quiet and dignified Sir Henry, whose only son was several months her senior.

'Surprisingly enough she adapted very quickly to married life, and settled down well in Devonshire. No matter what impression she may have given last night, she was touchingly devoted to Sir Henry, and utterly heartbroken when he died. She's still a relatively young woman, and I would like to think that she might one day marry again and have children, but I wouldn't be at all surprised if she did not.' She gave an unexpected gurgle of laughter. 'It isn't likely that too many gentlemen would be willing to put up with my niece's madcap ways.'

Perhaps not, Robina thought, trying to quell the sudden acrid taste rising in her throat by swallowing a mouthful of coffee, but one gentleman certainly gave the distinct impression last night that he might be willing to try.

In an attempt to rid herself of the totally unexpected melancholy state of mind which was increasingly plaguing her of late, Robina decided to pay a call on her friend Olivia. She would have much preferred to venture forth on her own, but as she knew that the Dowager, whose complacency did not stretch so far as to approve of young ladies wandering about the streets of towns and cities on their own, would deplore such behaviour, Robina asked Nancy, the young parlour-maid, to accompany her.

She arrived at the fashionable house Olivia's new brother-in-law had hired for the duration of their stay in Brighton to discover that her friend had had a similar idea, and had gone out for a walk. Olivia's sister Beatrice, however, was at home and, delighted by the unexpected visit, ordered refreshments to be brought to the front parlour at once.

For a while they discussed yet again the startling events which had taken place in recent weeks in Northamptonshire, before they went on to talk about more recent news—Hester Perceval's surprising betrothal, and the engagements of several other of their mutual acquaintances. Beatrice then went on to laughingly remark that she didn't suppose for a moment that it would be too long before her very welcome visitor found herself well and truly caught in parson's mousetrap, a suggestion which caused the most uncomfortable ache in a certain region beneath Robina's ribcage.

She swiftly assured her charming hostess that she had formed no attachment, and that it was much more likely that Olivia would be the next one to find herself engaged, a suggestion which instantly brought a troubled look into the new Lady Ravensden's eyes.

Robina was well aware that Beatrice was no fool, and that she had probably been aware for as long as Robina had herself that Olivia had been showing a marked interest in a certain Captain Jack Denning.

Having by this time met the gentleman on several occasions, Robina had decided that she rather liked him. He was undoubtedly handsome, and every young girl's idea of the dashing storybook hero, she supposed, which made her momentarily ponder anew on why she, unlike her friend Olivia, had never been particularly attracted to him.

There was no denying that he had a darkly brooding air. He had earned himself the reputation of being abrupt on occasion, and there had also been considerable gossip in certain quarters concerning a rift between himself and other members of his family which, quite naturally, might cause Beatrice some concern, if she supposed that her young sister's affections were genuinely engaged.

This, however, was none of her affair, even though she did consider herself a friend of the family, and she had no intention of prying or becoming involved in matters which were really none of her concern. So she tactfully turned the conversation to less personal issues, and a short while later declared that it was time she took her leave.

Although declining Beatrice's kind invitation to await Olivia's return, Robina decided not to go directly back to Daniel's house, and took a detour through the centre of the town, which certainly pleased the young parlour-maid.

Nancy, it quickly became apparent, enjoyed nothing more than gazing through shop windows to stare with wide, admiring eyes at the beautifully trimmed dresses and bonnets. Robina, on the other hand, could work up little enthusiasm, and was in the process of trying to persuade her dawdling companion to increase her pace, when she heard her name being called in a bright, cheerful voice. Surprised, she turned to discover a very smart open carriage drawing to a halt a matter of a few yards away.

'Good day to you, Miss Perceval,' the instantly recognisable sole occupant of the carriage greeted her, as Robina approached. 'Can I tempt you to accompany me about the town. I intended to call on Aunt Lavinia, so shall see you safely home afterwards.'

To have refused would have seemed churlish. Furthermore, Lady Tolliver seemed genuinely pleased to see her. Robina wished she could have said the same, for Daniel's cousin had given her no reason whatsoever to take her in dislike.

Her conscience began to prick her, for she was very well aware that the Vicar of Abbot Quincey would have been most disappointed in his eldest daughter if he ever thought for a moment that she was capable of feeling antipathy without a very good reason.

'I should be delighted to accept,' she responded, desperately striving to sound as though she truly meant it, and then turned to the young maid, who declared that she was more than happy to continue walking, providing Miss Perceval had no objection.

'Just like the maids back home,' Arabella declared, after ordering her coachman to move on. 'They all seem to derive a great deal of pleasure from gaping into shop windows. Quite understandable, I suppose! Most young women enjoy looking at frills and furbelows.' Her eyes narrowed as she suddenly subjected her companion to a penetrating stare. 'You, on other hand, did not appear to be enjoying yourself.'

Robina, returning that steady gaze, realised suddenly that Lady Tolliver and the Dowager had much more in common than a mere family resemblance. Both ladies, it seemed, were acutely observant.

Deciding it might be wise not to attempt to deny it, she said, 'I had my fill of gazing into shops during my stay in London.' She shrugged. 'It is very nice to be able to wear and own pretty things, but I'm afraid I'm one of those people who cannot work up much enthusiasm for possessions, Lady Tolliver.'

'A rare female, indeed,' Arabella murmured, before suggesting that formality cease between them. 'I hope you will call me Arabella, for I fully intend to address you by your given name. I do so hate unnecessary reserve, so we may as well start as we mean to go on, don't you think?'

Evidently taking the silence for agreement, Arabella looked about her with interest. 'Good heavens!' she exclaimed, suddenly, catching sight of a familiar figure in a passing carriage. 'Isn't that

Lady Milverton? What a quiz of a hat!' Chuckling wickedly, she turned her attention back to Robina. 'So, how are you enjoying your stay in Brighton?'

'Very much. Both Daniel and his mother have been so very kind, giving up so much of their time to keep me entertained. Daniel has even taken the trouble to teach me how to handle the ribbons.'

Arabella appeared genuinely impressed. 'My, my, wonders will never cease! Daniel must indeed think highly of you, my dear, to permit you to handle his precious horses. He always flatly refused to allow me to take charge of the ribbons whenever we ventured out together in the past. And I'm positive he never allowed his wife to drive herself about. Not that Clarissa would ever have considered learning how to handle a spirited pair,' she went on to divulge. 'Her interests, I'm afraid, were very limited.'

There had been no hint of malice in Arabella's voice. She had sounded quite matter-of-fact when disclosing those latter details, and yet something told Robina that Lady Exmouth had possibly been right when she had suggested that Arabella had not held the late Lady Exmouth in the highest esteem. It was also quite possible that Arabella had, indeed, secretly hoped to marry Daniel, and had resented the woman who had thwarted her ambition.

'You knew Daniel's late wife quite well, I understand,' she ventured in an attempt to discover a little more.

'Ha! So dear Aunt Lavinia has been discussing me, has she,' Arabella responded, a little knowing smile tugging at her full lips. 'She would! Yes, I knew Clarissa very well. I frequently paid visits to her home whenever I stayed at Courtney Place. We rubbed along together extremely well considering we had little in common. I was very much the tomboy, and enjoyed nothing better than climbing trees, and getting into all sorts of mischief, whereas dear Clarissa was very much the demur, young lady, quite happy to pass all her spare time sewing or drawing, or sitting at the pianoforte.'

The full lips curled into yet another effortless smile. 'She was certainly far more proficient at the so-called female accomplishments than I ever was, or ever could be for that matter,' she freely admitted. 'But she displayed precious little enthusiasm for much else, except perhaps socialising. Clarissa enjoyed being the centre of attention. To give her her due she wasn't in the least vain, but, I suppose, being so strikingly lovely, she had grown accustomed over the years to being the object of almost every gentleman's attention.'

She sighed, and after a moment added, 'Perhaps it was for the best that she died when she did. Her looks would undoubtedly have faded in time, and she would, I very much fear, have turned into one of those devilishly dull faded beauties who spend all their time lying on a couch, imagining that they have every sort of illness, while enjoying the doting attention of some foolish female companion.'

She laughed suddenly, an infectious gurgle that surprisingly had Robina chuckling too. 'Dear me, how old cattish I sound! Anyone listening to me would imagine that I disliked Clarissa, whereas in fact I liked her very well. She was immensely sweet and kind, and of course very, very lovely. I was not in the least surprised when Daniel became infatuated. Most gentlemen who met her fell instantly under her spell. But I was very surprised when he decided to marry her…I wonder how long it took him before he realised his mistake?'

Robina gaped in astonishment. Fortunately Arabella's attention was once again claimed by an acquaintance waving to her from a passing carriage, and by the time she turned back, Robina had succeeded in schooling her features.

'I must say, it is good to see Daniel enjoying life again. I wasn't able to attend Clarissa's funeral,' Arabella disclosed, glancing briefly at the golden band on her left hand. 'Dear Henry was fading fast at the time. He never fully recovered from that final attack, and died just a few months after Clarissa. Daniel came to his funeral. I was deeply shocked at the change in him. Now he seems a completely different man, happier than I've seen him look in years, I'm pleased to say. Though why in heaven's name I should continue to concern myself about the wretched creature I'll never know!'

Dark eyes, twinkling with mischief, turned towards Robina again. 'He's dragging my dear Roderick off to watch some fearful bout of fisticuffs the day after tomorrow, and leaving me quite without a protector. But I flatly refuse to wait at home for their return, so I've decided to organise an alfresco breakfast at some picturesque spot. Do say you'll make up one of the party. I'm determined to get to know you a good deal better, and determined too, that we shall become firm friends.'

Robina was not so very certain that they would ever become that close, and was even less certain why she felt that it might be wise to remain a little aloof where Lady Tolliver was concerned, for she was undeniably a most likeable woman whose innate honesty Robina could not help but admire.

* * *

That evening, when she saw Arabella again at a party given by yet another of the Dowager's close acquaintances, Robina began to feel even less inclined to make a friend of the lively widow.

When Lady Exmouth had mentioned, just before setting out, that she had received a note from her son expressing his regret that he now found himself unable to act as their escort, Robina had thought it most strange, for she had long since considered Daniel a man of his word. When he had pledged to do a certain thing, he invariably did do it.

As she entered Lady Maitland's stylish drawing-room, however, she understood fully why he had decided to break his word. There he stood, looking remarkably relaxed and happy, amidst a small group surrounding his lively cousin. There was no sign of Arabella's stepson, Sir Roderick, amongst the guests, and so Robina naturally assumed that Arabella had called upon her cousin's services to escort her to the party and, seemingly, he had been only too willing to oblige.

Robina could feel that unholy resentment returning again with a vengeance, and seemed powerless to check it. She knew she was reacting like some overindulged child to feel so aggrieved. Daniel had every right to escort whomsoever he chose.

She was painfully aware, too, that she was being thoroughly selfish in begrudging him time with his cousin, but for some obscure reason she couldn't help feeling as she did.

She tried her level best to appear pleased to see him when he did eventually notice their presence and came across the room to greet them, but it was an effort, and it showed. Daniel instantly detected the faint brittle note in her voice, and asked outright if she was feeling quite well.

'Yes, dear, you do look a little flushed,' the Dowager put in before Robina could assure him that she was perfectly all right. 'I sincerely trust you haven't taken Lady Phelps's chill. What an inconsiderate creature Augusta has become! Fancy paying morning calls when one's eyes and nose are streaming, and one is forever sneezing! I wouldn't be at all surprised if we are not both forced to take to our beds within the next few days.'

Aware that if she remained, she might foolishly betray the resentment she seemed powerless to control, Robina scanned the room, frantically searching for a means of escape, and thankfully discovered one. 'Oh, there's Olivia Roade Burton, with her sister. I paid a visit to them this morning, but unfortunately Olivia had gone out. Would you both excuse me whilst I go and have a word with my friend? I haven't seen her for days.'

'Are you certain she's all right, Mama?' Daniel enquired, the instant Robina had scurried away. 'She seems a little tense to me.'

'If that is so, then it is quite evident that where Miss Perceval is concerned you are a deal more observant than I am, my son,' she responded, beaming with satisfaction. 'She was fine earlier. As she mentioned, she went out for a walk this morning, and was brought safely home by dear Arabella. Nothing untoward has happened this day, I assure you.'

But Daniel was not at all convinced. He had made too close a study of her in recent weeks not to be certain that something had occurred to disturb the calm waters of her mind, something which, unless he much mistook the matter, she was determined to keep to herself.

Leaving his mother happily conversing with several acquaintances, he wandered into the room set out for cards, selecting a seat near the door from where he was able to view proceedings taking place back in the drawing-room.

Robina, being an extremely pretty girl, had never been short of invitations to step out on to the floor, and this evening proved no exception.

Each time Daniel raised his eyes from the cards in his hand it was to discover her lightly moving about the room, executing the steps of the various dances with effortless grace. On the surface at least she appeared to be enjoying herself hugely, but he was not fooled. Her smiles, he had noticed, lacked that certain spontaneous warmth, and there was just a hint of tension about the set of those lovely, gently sloping white shoulders.

Declining the invitation to play yet another hand, he eventually wandered back into the drawing-room in time to see her latest partner returning her to the protection of the Dowager's side. 'I hope you will do me the honour of saving me the supper dance?' he asked, coming upon her completely unobserved and making her start. 'And, of course, permit me to escort you in to supper afterwards.'

Robina made not the least attempt to conceal either her delight or surprise. Daniel, although an excellent dancer for a man of his size, and surprisingly light on his feet, took a turn on the floor only rarely, declaring that, having almost attained the ripe old age of six-and-thirty, he considered it far more dignified to watch the spectacle rather than take any part in it himself.

That he had chosen to escort her in to supper in preference to his cousin brought immense satisfaction, and she only hoped the invitation was not by way of recompense for failing to escort her to the party, but because he genuinely desired her company.

The smile she bestowed upon him while accepting the invitation came effortlessly to her lips, but it quite failed to persuade him to remain by her side, and he wandered away directly afterwards to join a group of friends congregating by the door.

On several occasions, as the evening progressed, Robina just happened to catch him staring in her direction, but he made no attempt to approach her again. Nor did he appear at her side to claim her hand shortly before the supper dance was due to begin.

'Do you happen to know where Daniel is hiding himself, ma'am?' she asked the Dowager, after scanning the room in a vain attempt to catch a glimpse of his tall, athletic figure.

'No, dear. I'm afraid I don't, unless he's still outside with Arabella. I thought I noticed them wandering out to the terrace a little earlier.'

Robina hesitated, but only for a moment. After all, it could do no harm to go in search of him, she told herself, making her way across to the tall French windows, which their thoughtful hostess had ordered to be left wide open to allow much needed fresh air into the room.

She was surprised to discover the terrace quite deserted, and turned, about to go back inside and search elsewhere, when a trill of feminine laughter floated up from the garden on the sweetly perfumed night air.

Her soft slippers made not a sound as she walked across the terrace towards the four stone steps leading down to a sizeable lawn. The two figures, silhouetted in the moonlight and standing close together, a mere few yards away, certainly appeared to remain oblivious to her presence. Despite the semi-darkness she had little difficulty in identifying them both, even before that easily recognisable female voice, heartbreakingly clear and carrying, announced, 'Oh, Daniel! I cannot tell you how happy that makes me! To think after all these years you have at last come to your senses... You have made the right choice this time, I think.'

Robina felt suddenly icy-cold, numb. Had she misheard...? Could she possibly have misunderstood? Then, as she watched Arabella wrapping her arms about that tall, muscular frame, and saw Daniel's willing response to the loving embrace, she could delude herself no longer.

Never before had Robina experienced so much gratitude towards her mother for insisting on such high standards of behaviour in her offspring than she did in those moments when the numbness began to leave her and her whole body was suddenly racked by the most agonising pain. Those strict lessons, instilled in her from childhood, could not be easily forgotten, and thankfully gave her the strength to suppress the agonised cry which rose in her throat, and to walk silently back into the house, dry-eyed, head held high, her unusual pallor the only indication that all was not well with her.

Nevertheless the distinct lack of colour didn't escape Lady Exmouth's notice, when at last she returned to her side. 'My dear, are you sure you feel quite the thing? You look quite dreadfully pale.'

'No, I do not feel very well, ma'am,' Robina answered, wondering how she could possibly manage to sound so natural when her throat felt as though it were being slowly squeezed by merciless fingers of steel. 'I have developed the most atrocious headache, and think it would be best if I leave at once.'

Lady Exmouth required no further prompting. But as Robina took her seat beside her in the carriage a few minutes later, thankfully escaping without having to face Daniel again, she was brutally aware that she would never be able to escape from the depths of her own feelings.

Chapter Nine

'Grateful though I've been for your generous hospitality, and unrivalled masculine company, I think the time has now come for me to return to my own abode,' Daniel suddenly announced to his friend, as they paused in their stroll about the town to study half a dozen or so small fishing boats heading out to sea.

The Honourable Mr Montague Merrell didn't attempt to dissuade him. 'I expected you to go several days ago. It's been quite apparent to me for some considerable time that you're head-over-heels in love with the chit. Miss Perceval's a dashed lovely girl. I really cannot understand why you've delayed this long.'

'You above anyone else should know why caution has become a byword with me, Monty. I've fallen in love before, remember?'

Easily detecting the slightly bitter note in the pleasantly mellow voice, Mr Merrell cast his companion a sympathetic look as they moved on to continue their exploratory stroll about the town. 'You were very young, Daniel,' he reminded him. 'I know at the time I numbered amongst the few who were against your marrying, but that was simply because I considered it would have been wise to wait a year or two. Looking back, I cannot recall a single gentleman of my acquaintance who wasn't instantly bewitched by Clarissa. And believe me I was no exception.'

'Maybe not... But at least you, my dear friend, had the sense to know the difference between infatuation and love, whereas I...'

Daniel didn't attempt to finish what he was saying. There was absolutely no need for him to do so, for his companion was the only person in whom Daniel had ever confided; the only one to have been furnished with all the unsavoury facts concerning the late Lady Exmouth's unexpected demise.

Automatically keeping pace with his friend, as they turned down one of Brighton's many side streets to explore a part of the town where he at least had never ventured before, Daniel cast his mind back to one particular evening, shortly after

Clarissa's funeral, when he had sat in the library at Courtney Place and had felt the need to confide in his friend Montague. He had openly confessed for the first time ever that his marriage had not been an unrivalled success, before he had gone on to relate all the details of Clarissa's tragic death. Daniel clearly recalled that his friend had looked genuinely shocked. Montague might have experienced reservations about his friend's marrying in the first place, but he, like everyone else, had believed the Exmouths' union had been a happy and successful one.

He cast his pensive companion a fleeting glance as they turned into yet another unfamiliar side street. 'Come on, Monty. Why don't you say, "I told you so." It's what's been passing through your mind, after all.'

'It most certain has not!' Merrell assured him, before a rueful smile tugged at one corner of his full lips. 'In point of fact, I was just thinking how very adept you've become over the years at hiding your feelings. I doubt there are half a dozen people residing in Brighton at the moment who might suspect that your feelings towards Miss Robina Perceval go rather deeper than that of mere friendship.'

'Yes, I have been most successful in my endeavours,' Daniel agreed, experiencing no small degree of satisfaction.

Montague regarded him in silence for a moment, and then asked, 'But surely you do not still harbour any doubts? Miss Robina Perceval is a darling girl, utterly delightful! I told you long before we left the capital that I considered that she would make you the ideal mate.'

'And you certainly ensured that you were given ample opportunity to form that opinion, as I remember,' Daniel returned, clearly recalling those occasions during the Season in London when he had chanced upon his friend seated in some secluded corner, conversing quietly with Robina. 'I might easily have been roused to a fit of jealous rage if I hadn't been quite certain that a confirmed old bachelor like yourself posed no threat.'

'And neither, from what I have witnessed during recent weeks, does anybody else,' Montague assured him, slanting a mocking glance. 'So why have you deliberately refrained from making your intentions perfectly plain?'

'Because, my dear inquisitive friend, I considered the time was not right, and that it certainly could do no harm to delay a few more weeks. Not for my benefit,' he went on to disclose. 'I had made my mind up to marry Robin long before we left the capital.'

That slightly rueful smile tugged at his lips once again. 'When, towards the end of last year, I first began to consider the suggestion put forward by several members of my family and many of my friends, including your good self, that I should marry again, I was thinking only of my daughters, not of myself. I finally decided that if I could find a female of good birth and gentle manners who would make a kind stepmother, and who would run my home efficiently, I would then seriously contemplate a second marriage. Needless to say, love never entered into my thinking… Then I came to London and met the Vicar of Abbot Quincey's daughter.'

'And instantly everything changed,' Montague suggested, but Daniel, truthful to the last, shook his head.

'No, not immediately. Not for several weeks, as it happens,' Daniel surprisingly confessed. 'Oh, I liked her very well from the start. She was precisely what I was looking for—pleasing on the eye, unspoiled and sweet-natured. Furthermore, she had three younger sisters, and so was quite accustomed to caring for young girls. I became determined to get to know her better, and in doing so discovered, much to my utter astonishment, that the unimaginable had happened and that I had grown inordinately fond…' Again the rueful smile flickered. 'No, let us be totally honest—I was astounded to discover that against all the odds I had fallen in love. And not just with a lovely face this time. None the less, I was very well aware that, although my mother was very much in favour of the match, and was doing everything within her power to promote it, as was Robina's own mama, Robina herself…'

'Oh, come man! The girl simply adores you,' Montague assured him in a voice that clearly revealed that he at least was in no doubt. 'That lovely young face of hers positively lights up whenever you're nearby.'

Daniel's expression softened, and a warm glow sprang into his dark eyes. 'Recently I have begun to think that perhaps she's starting to see me in something more than the light of just a friend.'

'I'm positive you're right. So what's holding you back, for heaven's sake?'

'Oh, I don't know.' Removing his beaver hat, Daniel ran impatient fingers through his hair, as he took stock of their surroundings for the first time. 'Where in the name of heaven are we?' His eyes came to rest on a tavern on the opposite side of the narrow street. 'Let's go in there. Dashed thirsty work all this aimlessly walking about!'

Montague, wrinkling his long nose in distaste, followed willy-nilly into the tavern. It wasn't quite up to the standard to which he had grown accustomed, but he found the home-brewed ale very palatable, and was content to remain for a short while in order to sample more.

After seating himself beside Daniel on one of the rough wooden settles, he wasn't slow to return to their former topic. 'So, how much longer do you intend to wait before popping the question?'

'Inquisitive devil!' Daniel admonished, but without rancour. How could one resent the curiosity of someone who had only one's best interests at heart, someone who had remained touchingly loyal and had been an unfailing support when one had needed it most?

'As a matter of fact I had made up my mind to propose last night.' His forehead suddenly creased with a slightly troubled frown. 'Unbeknown to me, my mother decided to leave the party early. I spent some time with my cousin Arabella in the garden, and when I returned to the house I was informed by our hostess that Miss Perceval had not been feeling too well and that my mother had taken her home. I called at the house this morning, but Robina was keeping to her room. My mother seems to think that she may have contracted a chill, but I'm not so sure.' He shrugged. 'She certainly didn't seem quite herself last night, but I wouldn't have said she was ill.'

'Probably just one of those mild female complaints,' his friend suggested. 'She'll recover soon enough, I dare say.'

Daniel cast him a faintly mocking glance. 'And what would a confirmed old bachelor like yourself know about women's troubles, may I ask?'

'A great deal more than you may think, old fellow,' Montague responded, with a distinctly self-satisfied smirk. 'I may never have been tempted into parson's mousetrap, but I ain't lived the life of a monk. The single state suits me very well, whereas it doesn't suit you, my friend. So do something about it! It ain't like you to be so indecisive.'

'I do not doubt the depth of my own feelings, Monty,' Daniel assured him after a moment's intense thought, 'but I cannot help wondering whether I am quite the right sort of person to make my little bird happy. Good God, man!' he exclaimed in response to his friend's derisive snort. 'She's nearer to my daughter Hannah's age than mine...Lizzie's, come to that!'

'Well, and what of it?' Montague responded, not considering the difference in ages in any way significant. 'You're in the prime of life—healthy, strong, a fine figure of a man.' He gazed down a little despondently at his own slightly thickening girth. 'I'm forced to admit that you're in far better shape than I am.'

'Maybe so, but that doesn't alter the fact that I'm fast approaching middle age. I enjoy a quiet life, and maybe am a little too staid and set in my ways for Robina's taste.'

His features adopted a certain wistful expression as he stared down into the contents of his tankard. 'In many ways we are very alike, very compatible, both seeming to enjoy the same sorts of things. But that doesn't alter the fact that she is still a deal younger than I am, with a young heart that craves a little excitement from time to time.

'Believe me, it is so,' he reiterated when his friend looked faintly sceptical. 'To all outward appearances she seems very demure, every inch the well brought up young lady, but hidden beneath the surface lurk quite amazing qualities. She's an intrepid little thing, which she proved when she saved my daughter from drowning, for which I shall be eternally in her debt. She's always keen to attempt new things, too, which sets her quite apart from most other young females of her class who are quite content to remain indoors, plying their needles.'

He paused for a moment, recalling clearly a certain conversation he had had with Robina on the night they had dined at the Pavilion. 'Although her upbringing was on the whole a happy one, her life at the vicarage lacked adventure, and there is a certain part of her that yearns to meet the kind of man who could rectify this deficiency in her life before she settles down to a quiet married life.'

'Well, why don't you then?' Monty suggested.

'And how the deuce do you propose I do that?' Daniel returned, a hint of exasperation creeping into his voice, making it carry further than he realised. 'I am not quite the swashbuckling type. Nor a knight in shining armour to ride *ventre a terre* to a damsel's rescue, even if the situation arose, which is highly improbable.'

'I'm not suggesting you wait for an opportunity to display your manly prowess, I'm suggesting you create one.'

'It is my considered opinion,' Daniel responded, casting his friend a faintly impatient glance, 'that that home-brewed ale has gone to your head.'

'Not a bit of it!' Montague assured him, laughing. 'Nothing could be easier. Simply arrange for dear little Robina to be abducted and then go gallantly dashing to her rescue. Tomorrow will do perfectly,' he went on, warming to the subject. 'She's to be amongst the guests invited to your cousin's alfresco breakfast out at Priory Wood, if my memory serves me correctly. The perfect opportunity for you to carry out the feat of daring.'

Daniel raised his eyes ceilingwards. 'A more addle-brained suggestion I have yet to hear!' he muttered. 'Even if I thought you were serious, which I know you're not, you don't suppose for a moment I'd lend myself to such a start.'

'Faint-hearted fellow!'

'Furthermore,' Daniel continued, ignoring the criticism, 'there is every likelihood that Robina will excuse herself from the outing. And even if she does decide to attend, there's not the remotest possibility that I could arrange her abduction in so short a time, even if I were foolish enough to contemplate doing such a senseless thing.'

He rose to his feet. 'Come, let us be gone from here, and trust that the fresh air will not be long in restoring your wits.'

Daniel turned, about to lead the way out of the inn, when he promptly collided with a small stocky individual who had been supping his ale at the very next table, and found himself on the receiving end of a rather direct, penetrating stare.

'Begging your pardon, guv'nor,' the stranger muttered, hurriedly stepping to one side. 'Didn't notice you standing there. No offence intended.'

'And none taken. It was as much my fault as yours,' Daniel responded, ever the polite gentleman.

It was only later, after he had arrived back at his friend's lodgings, that Daniel noticed his fob-watch was missing.

Trying not to dwell on the loss of a possession which he valued highly, simply because it was the last present his rapidly ailing father had bestowed upon him, Daniel accompanied his friend to a certain establishment where gambling for high stakes was the norm.

Mr Merrell, unlike Daniel himself, was a compulsive gambler, and was never happier than when seated at a table, glass of fine old brandy at his elbow, cards in his hand, pitting his skill against other gamesters. Considering he always played for high stakes, it was perhaps fortunate that Lady Luck had seen fit to favour him thus far. He certainly lost large sums on occasions, but never appeared unduly worried, for he felt certain that that beloved, fickle 'lady' would smile favourably upon him again before too long.

Daniel, standing behind his friend's chair, watched the play for a time, and then drifted away to enjoy a hand or two of piquet with an acquaintance. He distinctly lacked the faith in Lady Luck which his friend Montague possessed, and decided after half an hour to leave and seek out his mother who had planned to attend a large party being held at a house nearby.

The hostess, a friend of the family's for many years, was delighted by his unexpected appearance. After a brief exchange of pleasantries, Daniel did not delay very long in searching out his mother, and discovered to his intense disappointment that she had come to the party alone.

'Although Robina insisted that there was absolutely no need to summon the doctor, she didn't feel equal to accompanying me this evening,' her ladyship disclosed. 'I believe she has every intention of joining us on the picnic tomorrow, however.'

'If she feels well enough, then of course she may, but if not, do not hesitate to summon the doctor.'

The Dowager recognised that decisive note in her son's voice. Like his father before him, Daniel was a most charming, level-headed man, but could be quite determined and authoritative when the need arose. She smiled up at him. 'And have you definitely decided to return to us tomorrow, my dear?'

'Yes. I've given orders for my belongings to be taken back to the house during my absence. As you know, I've arranged to spend the day with Roderick. I expect to return to Brighton early in the evening, and will come directly to the house.'

Leaving his mother to return to her friends, he wandered about the room, stopping from time to time to converse with several acquaintances, but Robina's absence meant there was little inducement for him to remain, and he soon took himself off, deciding to have an early night as he had an early start in the morning.

Declining the footman's offer to find him a hired carriage, Daniel walked the relatively short distance back to his friend's lodgings, arriving just as a church clock somewhere in the distance chimed the hour. As he waited for his friend's very efficient manservant to admit him to the house, he thought he detected someone lurking in the shadows on the opposite side of the street. He paid little attention, however, and went straight into the house as soon as the door had been opened, taking himself into the library for a nightcap before finally retiring to his room.

No sooner had he poured himself a brandy than the sound of the door-knocker echoed in the small hall. To him it seemed a very odd time for someone to decide to pay a call, and therefore made no attempt to hide his surprise when the servant entered a minute or so later to inform him that there was a person at the door wishing to see him.

'What sort of person?'

Mr Merrell's very correct manservant sniffed loudly. 'A very common sort, my lord. He came to the house earlier whilst you were out. I would not have hesitated to send him about his business had it not been for the fact that he informed me that he had in his possession some property belonging to you.'

'Has he, indeed?' Daniel murmured, his thoughts automatically turning to the missing watch.

'So I am led to believe, sir. When I suggested that he might safely hand whatever it was over to me, he stubbornly refused to do so, declaring that he would place it in your hands personally, or not at all.'

'In that case, you'd better show the fellow in,' Daniel suggested, and a few moments later a small, stocky individual wearing a serviceable frieze coat, and twisting a somewhat battered and misshapen hat round and round in his hands, entered the room.

Daniel had a remarkable memory for faces, and instantly recognised the individual with whom he had momentarily collided in the inn that afternoon. 'So, we meet again, Mr—er…?'

'Higgins, sir. Honest Hector Higgins, at your service.'

'It is to be hoped, Mr Higgins, that you live up to your name,' Daniel remarked in a distinctly sardonic tone, as he gazed at the work-roughened fingers, which looked hard and clumsy, but which might well be nimble enough to remove an article from someone's pocket without the owner being any the wiser. 'You are in possession of an item belonging to me, I understand.'

'That I am, sir.' Delving into his pocket, Higgins drew out the treasured possession and promptly placed it into Daniel's outstretched hand.

He examined it briefly, noting with some relief that it was completely undamaged. 'It would seem, Master Higgins, that I am in your debt. Or at least I would be if I were not fairly certain that you quite expertly purloined this from my waistcoat pocket during our brief—er—contact in that inn.'

A decidedly wary expression flickered momentarily over the weather-beaten features. 'Now, guv'nor, I puts it to you…if I'd filched the watch, I wouldn't be giving it back, now would I?'

'You might if you thought you would attain more by way of reward than you would by trying to dispose of it by other means, especially as my name is clearly engraved in the back.'

'Pshaw! It'd be no bother to scratch that away, and no one none the wiser,' Higgins responded, determined, it seemed, to brazen it out. 'And I didn't bring it back 'ere, personal like, for no reward neither. I'm an 'onest cove. Weren't always, I'm ashamed to say, but I is now, and 'ave been since I met my Dora.'

Daniel couldn't help smiling at this artless disclosure, and was inclined to be generous and give the fellow the benefit of the doubt. 'That being the case, Master Higgins, and as you seem disinclined to accept a reward, the least I can offer you is a drink for your trouble.' He turned to the decanters. 'Will brandy serve?'

'Mighty hospitable of you, guv'nor. Yes, that'll do very nicely.'

Smiling in spite of the fact that he still strongly suspected that some recompense would be demanded for the safe return of the watch, Daniel obligingly poured a large measure of brandy and handed it to his visitor.

'Sit yourself down, Higgins, and tell me about yourself. What do you do for a living?'

'I'm a jarvey, sir. Been driving me own carriage these past ten year or more.' He sniffed, wiping his snub nose on the back of his hand. ''Course, the carriage is getting a bit worn and battered now, and the poor old 'orse ain't what she was.' He shook his head sadly. 'No, won't be long before she pays a visit to the knacker's yard.'

'How very unfortunate!' his lordship said faintly, wondering what in the world had possessed him to invite the visitor to remain.

'Aye, sir. It ain't easy being an 'onest cove. Gentry folk don't like to be seen driving about in a broken-down old carriage like mine, and when you don't pick up many passengers in a day, you can't afford repairs.'

'I sympathise with your plight, Higgins,' Daniel responded, wondering when the despondent jarvey would disclose his real motive for this visit. He did not have long to wait.

'Knew you would, sir.' His eyes never wavering from Daniel's face, he consumed the contents of his glass in one go. 'Just like a soft-hearted cove like myself can sympathise with yours.'

Daniel took a sip from his own glass. 'I'm sorry, Higgins. I do not perfectly understand you.'

'Unrequired love, sir, can do terrible things to a man.'

'I'm sure you're right,' his lordship responded, while manfully suppressing a chuckle. 'But I believe you mean unrequited love.'

'Aye, that's it, guv'nor! But don't you be a'fretting no longer, 'cause Hector Higgins be the man to 'elp you there.'

Daniel blinked several times, wondering if he could possibly have misheard. 'I'm sorry, Higgins, I do not perfectly understand you. I am not in need of help.'

'Now, now, guv'nor, there's no need for you to be ashamed of yer feelings. Comes to us all in time. It 'appened to me, and now it's 'appened to you. Not that I likes to interfere, you understand, but I couldn't 'elp overhearing that little talk you had with your friend in the Crown, and knew I was the very man you was looking for.'

Daniel was becoming faintly bored, and it clearly showed as he said, 'And what service, pray, do you suppose you can render me?'

'Why, abducting the wench o' course! I knows the area round Priory Wood like the back of me 'and. Nowt could be simpler! All I needs to do is lurk in the woods tomorrow, awaiting the opportunity, like, nab the wench, and bung 'er in me carriage. Then you comes riding along, brandishing yer pistol. Mind, I wouldn't advise you discharge the firearm, m'lord,' he went on in all seriousness. 'Might frighten the old 'orse, and she ain't as young as she was. Might be too much for 'er.' He paused to cast a hopeful glance down at his empty glass. 'Now, what's do you think to that, m'lord?'

Daniel regarded him in silence for a moment, much as he might have done some half-witted child. 'I think, Master Higgins, that you have taken leave of your senses. Even if this plan of yours was not ludicrous in the extreme, I would still never countenance such a dishonourable act as abducting a young female and frightening her half out of her wits. Furthermore, what you overheard earlier today was my friend allowing the sportive element in his nature to get the upper hand, which he is sometimes inclined to do, but believe me his idiotic suggestion was never meant to be taken seriously. Unlike the one I am about to make, which is that we both seek our beds.'

In one graceful movement, Daniel rose from his chair, and relieved his highly disappointed visitor of the empty glass. 'Now, Master Higgins, I shall bid you goodnight... And consider yourself lucky that I'm not taking the little matter of the deliberate purloining of my watch any further.'

As the Dowager Lady Exmouth knew very well, there was an element of hard determination in her son's character which surfaced from time to time. It was clearly discernible now. Higgins opened his mouth to speak, thought better of it, and went disconsolately across to the door. 'No offence intended, m'lord,' he muttered over his shoulder and then, manfully resisting the temptation to place a well-aimed punch on the disdainful manservant's long nose, did not delay in leaving the house.

Life could be so unfair, he decided, as he trudged his weary way homewards. Here was he, an honest cove, doing honest work week in week out; year in year out. And for what? Hardly earning enough to keep body and soul together, he reflected, his spirits plummeting to an all-time low. He would be better off by far if he returned to his former profession... But no, he'd promised his Dora that his thieving days were over. He'd left that life behind him when he had moved away from London, and he had no real desire to return to a life of crime.

Not that he couldn't if he'd a mind to be so foolish, he reminded himself. His fingers were still as nimble as ever they were. He'd managed to take that gent's watch without his knowing much about it, he mused, with a certain grim satisfaction. Not that he had ever intended to keep it, though. That had never crossed his mind for a moment. He shook his head sadly, swiftly deciding that, as things had turned out, he might have been wiser to have done so. After all, what had all his good intentions brought him…? Absolutely nothing!

'Ahh well,' he muttered, crossing the street and entering the tavern. At least he had a few coins left in his pocket, enough to buy a tankard of ale to drown his sorrows.

The Crown was unusually quiet that evening, which suited his present unsociable mood very well, and Higgins had little difficulty in finding himself a secluded table in a corner, where he could continue to brood over life's iniquities without interruption.

Fate, it seemed, had other ideas, and was not even gracious enough to grant him the brief period of solitude for which he craved, for no sooner had he made himself comfortable on the settle than a sharp-featured man, sporting a bright red neckerchief clumsily knotted about his throat, and a blowsy female, whose low-cut gown left little to the imagination, plumped themselves, uninvited, on the settle opposite.

‘’’Ere, what’s all this, Hector, me old friend? Ain’t like you to skulk away in a corner. Had a bad day, ’ave we?’ The man’s thin lips curled unpleasantly to reveal a set of rapidly decaying teeth. ‘Now me, I’ve ’ad a good day. Told you afore old friend that you want to join forces wi’ me.’

‘And I’ve told you before, Jack Sharpe, that I gave up that kind o’ life long since.’

‘Aye, and where’s it got yer, eh?’ The decaying teeth showed again. ‘Working all the hours God sends, and for what? I bet you ain’t enough in your pocket for another tankard of ale.’

This was true enough, but Higgins had no intention of admitting to it, especially not to an unscrupulous little sneak-thief like Jack Sharpe who didn’t care how he got his grubby fingers on money. He was not above sending his woman friend out on the streets, and living off her immoral earnings when he was without the price of a drink.

‘Still,’ Jack shrugged, ‘I don’t know why I’m bothering wi’ you. You wouldn’t be much ’elp to me n’ more. You’re not up to it no longer—too old and too slow.’

‘Oh, no I ain’t!’ the older man countered, the

goading just too much for him this time. 'I'll 'ave you know I filched a fine pocket-watch this very day. Had it off the waistcoat and into me own pocket in a trice, and the gent none the wiser.'

'Oh, yeah!' Jack's tone was decidedly sceptical. 'Where is it, then? Show it to me!'

'I ain't got it no longer,' Higgins mumbled, going slightly red in the face. 'I gave it back.'

'You did what!' Sharpe and his companion roared with laughter, making Higgins feel more uncomfortable than ever.

He took an uneasy glance about him. 'Keep your voice down, can't yer!' he snapped. 'Do you think I want everyone to hear?'

'Frightened your little wife wouldn't like it if she knew you'd been up to your old tricks again, is that it, eh?' the woman goaded, and Higgins cast her a look of distaste.

'Shut yer mouth, Molly!' Jack ordered, his gaze suddenly intense. 'I reckon old Hector 'ere ain't spinning no yarn. I reckon he did filch the timepiece. Though why in Hades 'e decides to give it back, I can't imagine.'

Half wishing now that he hadn't done so, and being made to feel incredibly stupid into the bargain, Higgins explained the reason behind his actions, relating the conversation which he had overheard earlier in the day and disclosing what had subsequently occurred.

Jack listened intently, absorbing every last detail. 'So, you actually went to this Lord Exmouth's house, hoping he'd agree to your plan, and he threw you out on your ear, did 'e?'

'No, not then,' Higgins countered. 'I told you, I went round to his 'ouse, round to the rear entrance, and discovered from the scatty kitchen wench that 'e weren't staying there. Only 'is mother and this wench he's got his heart set on is living in the 'ouse. He's staying with a friend. So I calls there, and the second time I goes, I sees 'im.'

'Pity he weren't interested,' Jack remarked, much to his female companion's intense amusement.

'Can't say I'm surprised!' she scoffed. 'If the gent's half as fond of this wench as you reckon 'e is, Hector, he wouldn't be so mean as to want 'er abducted in a broken-down old carriage like yourn. Why, I've travelled in the dratted thing m'self once, and I should know. Black and blue I was after I got back from me sister-in-law's funeral.'

'Shut yer gab, woman!' Jack growled. '''Ere, go and get us all another drink.' He tossed her a coin and waited for her to move away, before turning once again to Higgins.

'And you reckon this wench Lord Exmouth's a fancy for will be out at Priory Wood tomorrow?'

'I've already said so, haven't I?' He cast a suspicious glance across the table. 'Why are you so interested, anyhow?'

'No reason, I suppose.' There was a faint rasping sound as Jack rubbed his bony fingers back and forth across his chin. 'All the same, it's a damned shame the cove didn't take to the idea. Might 'ave been able to 'elp you out, there.'

Having had more than enough for one day, and more than enough of the present company, Higgins hurriedly tossed the contents of his tankard down his throat and rose to his feet. 'Thanks all the same, but I can do without your sort of 'elp, Jack Sharpe.'

'Oh! Hector gone, as 'e?' Molly remarked, as she returned, glasses in hand. 'Never mind, I'll soon drink 'is gin. The ungrateful dog!'

'Oh, no, you won't!' Jack whisked the glass from her fingers. 'You needs to be up bright and early in the morning. I've got a job for you.'

'Oh, yes?' She cast him a wary look. 'What kind of job?'

'I wants you to go to this Exmouth's house and

keep watch. If this wench goes to Priory Wood, I wants to know about it.'

'But I don't even know what she looks like,' Molly pointed out, not relishing the prospect of rising early. 'Besides not knowing where she lives.'

'You'll find out easy enough.' He was thoughtful for a moment. 'You 'eard what Higgins said. Apart from the servants, only Exmouth's old mother and the girl are staying at the 'ouse. You wait outside and keep watch.'

'Then what?'

'Your brother's place is close to Priory Wood, ain't it?'

'Wel...? And what of it?'

Jack leaned back against the settle. 'I'll tell you in the morning, when I've had chance to think about it some more.'

Chapter Ten

Lady Exmouth beamed with pleasure as she watched Robina, looking particularly enchanting in a powder-blue walking dress and matching pelisse, descending the stairs. She wished Daniel could have been there to witness the utterly charming spectacle. That lovely face, framed in a fetching bonnet, with its powder-blue ribbons tied in a coquettish bow beneath the delightfully pointed little chin, was a sight to take the most hardened gentleman's breath away.

Not that she thought for a moment that Daniel himself was in any need of further persuasion to convince him that Robina would make him the ideal wife. Unless she very much mistook the matter the wretched boy had made up his mind weeks before, no matter how hard he had tried to conceal the fact. And if any further proof of the exact state of his mind had been required, he had certainly betrayed himself the previous night, her ladyship decided, experiencing an immense feeling of satisfaction. Why, not even Arabella's presence could induce him to remain at the party. If Robina herself had been present, of course, it would have been a different matter entirely!

'Now, my dear, are you quite certain that you feel up to this outing today?' the Dowager enquired as Robina reached her side. The girl certainly appeared perfectly restored, if a little paler than the Dowager would have liked. 'It isn't too late to change your mind,' she assured her. 'Arabella will quite understand.'

'I'm fine, really,' Robina answered, making a great play of straightening a crease in one of her gloves. 'I cannot imagine what came over me. I'm not usually prone to those trifling megrims.'

'Well, we must just be thankful that it was nothing more serious than an annoying headache which refused to go away. Had you contracted Lady Phelps's chill you might have been laid up for days. I understand that Augusta, poor dear, is still keeping to her bed. Which means, of course, that we shall be denied her company, and that of her son's at the alfresco breakfast.'

Robina clearly detected the faint hint of relief in the Dowager's tone, but chose not to remark upon it, and merely enquired who else would be travelling out to Priory Wood that morning.

'I'm not perfectly certain, my dear. Several people we are both acquainted with, I'm sure. I do know Arabella invited Sir Percy Lovell, but he was otherwise engaged. And I do believe she asked that nice young man of whom you're so fond, Mr Frederick Ainsley, but he too was forced to decline. I understand he has left town for a few days in order to visit a sick relative.' She shook her head. 'It is so difficult to arrange these things at a moment's notice, but I'm certain Arabella will have succeeded in persuading several people to come.'

The Dowager raised one hand, encased in a lilac-coloured glove. 'Ah! That sounds suspiciously like her now.'

Lady Exmouth's hearing was not defective. The footman opened the door in time to see the Tollivers' elegant open carriage drawing to a halt outside, and Arabella herself on the point of alighting.

'There's no need for you to trouble yourself,' the Dowager called, hurrying down the steps to greet her. 'We're ready and waiting, so we can leave at once, if you're agreeable?'

'Splendid! I do so admire punctuality!' Arabella announced, seating herself once again. 'And Robina too! Glad to see you felt able to accompany us. You and I, I'm afraid, are the youngest members of the party, so must keep each other company,' she went on, when Robina, at a far more decorous pace, arrived at the carriage. 'I'm rather surprised that not too many young people chose to accept my invitation. It would seem, though, that outdoor entertainment appeals more to the older generation.'

'I thought you might not find it so very easy to arrange your little picnic at such short notice, my dear,' Lady Exmouth remarked, making herself comfortable in the seat beside her niece. 'I find people these days tend to plan their schedules well in advance. Evening events are particularly difficult to arrange at short notice. One discovers that even one's friends refuse on the grounds of having prior engagements.'

'And that is precisely why I didn't attempt to organise a dinner-party,' Arabella responded vaguely, her attention suddenly drawn to a solitary figure on the opposite side of the street.

'What an exceedingly rude female!' she announced. 'That young woman has been pointedly staring in this direction from the moment I arrived.' She laughed suddenly, her sense of humour coming to the fore. 'I sincerely trust she's not hoping to see Daniel. She'll have a very long wait if she is.'

The Dowager, after one glance across the street, sniffed loudly. 'My son, I'll have you know, does not associate with persons of that—er—ilk.'

'Don't be so naïve, Aunt!' That mischievous sparkle of old was back in Arabella's eyes. 'Clarissa has been dead for almost two years... Though perhaps you're right,' she went on, after considering the matter further for a moment. 'Daniel has more taste than to associate with such a lowly sort. Or, perhaps, more respect for his health.'

Reaching forward she gave her coachman the office to start by tapping him lightly on the shoulder with her parasol, and the coach moved off, leaving the inquisitive female, Robina noticed, watching their progress along the street.

Robina, at least, had not been so naïve as not to know precisely to what Lady Tolliver had been alluding. She had swiftly discovered during her stay in the capital that it was certainly not unusual for a gentleman, widowed or otherwise, to keep a mistress. Whether Daniel himself did so, she wasn't so certain; wasn't sure either why it should matter to her one way or the other. After all, she told herself, it was no concern of hers. It would have been very much her concern if she had been in Arabella's position, and yet Daniel's future wife did not appear in the least troubled. How very unnatural that seemed!

'You're very quiet.'

The unexpected remark startled Robina out of her reverie, and she raised her eyes to discover Lady Tolliver's brown orbs firmly fixed in her direction.

'I do trust Aunty did not bully you into accompanying us today?'

'No such thing!' Robina assured her, managing a semblance of a smile. 'I was merely woolgathering.'

Unable to hold that faintly unnerving dark-eyed scrutiny, all too reminiscent of Daniel's on occasions, she glanced skywards to discover not one single cloud lurking anywhere. 'I think you are going to be lucky with the weather. It looks set to be yet another fine day.'

'It certainly does,' she agreed. 'I just hope it doesn't become too warm. Still,' she shrugged, 'there ought to be plenty of shade out at Priory Wood.'

'I could have wished you had chosen a different

spot for your outing,' Lady Exmouth put in. 'My memories of that particular idyllic place are not altogether pleasant.'

Arabella frankly laughed. 'Yes, Daniel told me all about it. What a little monkey Lizzie is! Not in the least like her mother. She must take after our side of the family.'

Tutting, the Dowager favoured her sportive niece with a reproving glance, and Arabella tried to look suitably chastened. 'Yes, you're quite right, Aunt. It is exceedingly naughty of me to make light of the matter. Daniel, I know, was most disturbed by the whole incident.' She looked directly across at Robina once again. 'And eternally grateful to you, my dear. He quite openly admits that he shall be forever in your debt.'

Perhaps Arabella did not notice the touch of sadness which just for one unguarded moment clouded those strikingly pretty blue eyes, but the Dowager most certainly did, and couldn't help wondering if her charming protégée was quite as restored to health as she would have people believe. Arabella was the dearest creature imaginable, but she could be a little tactless on occasions, and faintly overpowering, most especially to those who were not feeling quite equal to coping with her exuberance.

So she deliberately set herself the task of holding her niece in conversation by enquiring precisely who might be expected to join them at the alfresco breakfast that morning. Robina certainly did her best to contribute from time to time to the ensuing discussion, but Lady Exmouth sensed that it was an effort, and she became increasingly convinced that Robina would have much preferred to remain at home.

If the Dowager had suspected for a moment just how much of a trial Robina was finding the outing, she would have been appalled. The considerable strain of trying to behave normally lessened, of course, when they eventually reached the popular beauty spot, and the other guests began to arrive. Then Robina was able, without she hoped making it too obvious, to disengage herself from Arabella's side. She even managed to force several of the delicious delicacies the Tollivers' excellent cook had taken the trouble to prepare down her throat. As soon as she was able to do so, however, she drifted away from the few members of the party who had not succumbed to the heat of the day and the effects of several glasses of cool champagne by taking a nap, and sought the solace for which she craved.

The instant she felt certain that no one had decided to follow her example by going for a stroll, Robina ventured further into the wood. The river, she knew, was some distance away to her left, but she had no intention of venturing anywhere near it. The memories of that day, of far happier times, were all too firmly embedded in her mind.

But that was all she would be left with soon, a cruelly taunting voice in her head reminded her: bittersweet memories and the painful knowledge that events might have turned out so vastly different if she hadn't remained for so many weeks so insensitive to the desires of her own heart.

Tugging at the bow beneath her chin, she removed her bonnet and, holding it by its ribbons, absently began to swing it to and fro as she ventured further beneath the dense canopy of trees, not quite ready yet to abandon this much needed period of solitude.

She had realised, of course, when she had agreed to accompany the Dowager today that she would not find Arabella's company easy to bear. She hadn't realised quite how painful an ordeal it would turn out to be. A sigh escaped her. But what choice had she? She could hardly remain skulking in her bedchamber indefinitely, giving way to bouts of weeping when she felt certain she wouldn't be disturbed. Daniel himself would be returning to the house that evening, and although it might be distressingly hard, sooner or later she would have to face him too.

No, she thought sadly, there would be no easy way out for her. The next few days, or until she could find some reasonable excuse to leave Brighton and return to Northamptonshire would be agonisingly tortuous. Today had been traumatic enough. Trying to be at least civil to someone whom one resented bitterly had been no easy task, and yet she could not find it within herself to hate Arabella, nor even remotely dislike her. How could she blame Arabella for feeling a deal of affection for Daniel? Any woman would wish to marry such a fine man.

That no mention had been made of the forthcoming marriage was rather odd, though, she decided, frowning slightly as this puzzling thought occurred to her. They might, of course, have reasons for wishing their betrothal not to become common knowledge. It was quite possible that Daniel wished to inform his daughters that he intended to remarry and was awaiting their return from Dorset before informing the world at large. It was still rather odd, though, that they had decided to keep their intentions a secret from the Dowager, for Robina felt certain that Lady Exmouth was completely ignorant of the fact that her son intended to wed again. Furthermore, Arabella had betrayed no obvious signs that a joyous event would very soon be taking place in her life. How very odd it all was!

The sound of hurrying footsteps nearby broke into her perplexing reflections. So, someone had chosen to follow her example, after all, she thought, swinging round to discover precisely which member of the party had seen fit to come in hot pursuit.

Setting his book to one side, Daniel consulted his pocket-watch, which informed him that it wanted only a few minutes to seven. His mother and Robina were rather late in returning from their alfresco breakfast. What an utterly ridiculous description to give a meal eaten early in the afternoon! he mused, returning the watch to his pocket and reaching for his book again.

The door opened, and the butler entered the library to set a decanter and a glass by his lordship's elbow. 'Shall you be requiring anything further, sir?'

'No, I don't think so, thank you, Stebbings… Yes, wait a moment,' he added, arresting the servant's progress across to the door. 'What time did her ladyship leave this morning?'

'Shortly before noon, sir.'

'Did she happen to mention that there was a possibility that she might be returning late?'

'No, my lord, she did not. Shall I delay dinner?'

'Yes, perhaps that might be wise. Inform Cook that we'll now eat at nine.'

Frowning slightly, Daniel reached for the burgundy at his elbow and poured himself a glass. It was most unlike his mother not to inform the servants if she thought there was a possibility that she might be late. What on earth could be keeping her? he wondered. Even if she had lost track of the time, there had been others present to remind her, most especially Robina who, unlike most females of his acquaintance, was an excellent little timekeeper.

Smiling to himself he leaned back in his chair, and sipped his wine while absently contemplating the shine on his Hessian boots. It was good to be back in his own home again. He had enjoyed his friend Monty's company very much, but he had missed not having his little bird around, missed her far more than he cared to admit.

What an unusual female his little Robin was! Never would he have believed it possible that in a simple country parson's daughter, whose upbringing had been, by her own admission, faintly constricted, and wholly conventional, he would have found a female so much after his own heart.

It had come as something of a revelation to discover just how much they did have in common. He could not prevent a further wry smile tugging at the corners of his mouth. To think that when he had first seriously begun to consider the idea of marrying again, his only objective had been to find a suitable mother for his daughters, and in doing so he had found the perfect life's companion, a female whom he was very sure he could no longer live without.

A sudden commotion in the hall disturbed these pleasurable musings, and he turned his head in time to see his mother burst into the room, with less than her usual grace, swiftly followed by his cousin who was looking unusually pale, and whose eyes distinctly lacked that teasing sparkle.

'Oh, Daniel, thank heavens you're here!' The Dowager almost fell upon his chest as he rose from the chair. 'It is all my fault. I blame myself entirely. I should never have taken her. I knew as soon as we set out that the poor child was not equal to the outing.'

'Now, Aunt Lavinia, you must not distress yourself so.' Placing her arm about the Dowager's shoulders, Arabella drew her across to the sofa. 'I'm certain there's some perfectly reasonable explanation for all this,' she said in a voice which, to Daniel's ears, sadly lacked any real conviction.

'Where is Robina?' he asked with deceptive mildness.

'That is just it, Daniel. We don't know,' Arabella answered, striving to remain calm. 'She has disappeared.'

His expression giving no hint of the anxiety rapidly rising within him, he transferred his gaze from his silently sobbing mother to his cousin. 'I think you had better explain precisely what has occurred.'

'What Aunt Lavinia said is perfectly true,' she began. 'Robina did seem unusually subdued today.' She shrugged. 'I thought, perhaps, it might be simply that there was no one of her own age at the picnic, and she was faintly bored. Which would have been in no way amazing. I was beginning to regret organising the wretched outing myself when most of my guests decided to take a nap after the meal. So when I noticed Robina wandering off into the wood, I was very tempted to join her.' She glanced down at the slightly misshapen, blue-trimmed bonnet she held in her right hand. 'Now, of course, I wish I had done just that.'

'So, when she failed to return, you quite naturally searched for her.'

Arabella watched him calmly reach for his wine, looking for all the world as though he hadn't a care. She, however, knew him rather too well to be fooled by this seeming display of unconcern, and couldn't help but admire the iron self-control he never failed to exert over himself in times of crisis.

'I thought at first that she had merely lost track of the time. I recall when I was younger I loved to wander through the wood at Courtney Place, and was frequently late in returning for meals. It was only when my guests began to depart that I really became concerned. Several of them offered to remain and join the search, but I assured them that there was no need.' She regarded him in silence for a moment. 'I didn't suppose that you'd want the whole of Brighton knowing that Robina had disappeared.'

A faint look of admiration sprang into his eyes. 'You acted very sensibly, Bella. Indeed I would not like the tattle-mongers to get wind of this.'

'No, I thought not. So, after everyone had gone,

I ordered my servants to search the wood thoroughly, and my footman found this.'

She held out the bonnet for his inspection. One of the ribbons had clearly been torn off, and there was what appeared to be part of a large footprint on the brim.

'I thought she might possibly have met with an accident—fallen and twisted her ankle, perhaps. I dispatched one of my servants to the village nearby to enquire whether a young woman had gone there seeking assistance, but…'

She raised deeply troubled eyes to his. 'Oh, Daniel, I do not believe I'm a fanciful woman, but it almost seems to me as though she has been abducted.'

The Dowager, who had managed to regain control over herself at last, looked up at this. 'But that's nonsense, Arabella! Who on earth would want to abduct the dear, sweet child? Besides, who could possibly have known, apart from the guests, that we intended to go to Priory Wood today?'

'Who indeed?' Daniel murmured, eyes narrowing to slits.

Then, turning abruptly, he went striding across to the door. 'Stebbings!' he called. 'I want my curricle brought round from the stables at once!'

Chapter Eleven

Robina turned her head in the direction of the small and decidedly grubby window to see the light was fading fast. How long had she lain here like this, trussed up like a chicken? And why had she been captured and imprisoned in this disgustingly filthy attic room in the first place?

It had all happened so quickly, too. One moment she had been ambling through that wood, minding her own business; and the next she had been accosted by two complete strangers. Before she had had time even to scream one of the men had grasped her arms and had tied them behind her back, while the other had wrapped a disgusting gag over her mouth. Then, after an evil-smelling sack had been flung over her head, she had been forced to suffer the indignity of being carried some distance across a brawny shoulder before being bundled none too gently into a cart.

By the jolting she had been forced to endure, they had obviously travelled along very uneven tracks. The journey had seemed to take forever, but she suspected she had travelled no more than three miles, if that. Then she had been carried in the same undignified manner up two flights of stairs and had been left here tied to this bed. Frowning, she looked about her. But where was here? Where on earth was she? More importantly, why was she here?

The sound of footsteps and voices interrupted these disturbing reflections. A moment later there was the noise of bolts being drawn back, the door swung open, and the two men who had abducted her came into the room, followed by a blowsy female whom Robina was convinced she had seen somewhere before.

'God's teeth, Jack!' the woman exclaimed, casting the captive a look of sympathy. 'Why did you leave her tied up like this?' Depositing the tray she carried down on a wooden box beside the bed, she began to undo the rope securing the slender ankles. 'How the devil do you suppose she can escape from up here?'

'It weren't me,' the smaller man answered testily. 'I left the tying up to yer brother.'

The woman cast the other man, who was leaning against the wall, and looking over at the bed with a decidedly lascivious gleam in his dark eyes, an impatient glance. 'She ain't no bird, Ben. She can't fly out of the window.'

'I weren't going to risk a pretty little morsel like that slipping through me fingers.' The leer became more pronounced. 'Don't gets the chance to 'andle such quality goods so often.'

'You can just keep your grubby 'ands to yerself, Ben,' the woman snapped, knowing precisely in which direction her brother's thoughts were turning. 'She ain't to be harmed. We all agreed on that.'

'Aye, and so we did,' Jack concurred, moving forward to help untie the rope binding their captive's slim wrists. 'It's the money we're after, nothing else.'

Robina, having listened to this little discussion with interest, was able to sit up at last, and wasted no time in pulling the filthy rag from round her mouth. At least she now knew why she had been abducted. She was being held for ransom. But why had they chosen her? Was it simply a case of being in the wrong place at the wrong time, and just happening to cross their paths? Or had she been their intended victim all along?

She looked at each of her captors in turn. The men she felt certain she had never seen before they had snatched her from the wood, but the woman she most definitely had. She studied her intently. Like Daniel, she had a remarkable memory for faces, and it didn't take many moments before she suddenly realised precisely where she had seen her.

'You were in the street this morning, watching the house.'

The woman didn't attempt to deny it. 'Well, I 'ad to make sure we nabbed the right one, now didn't I, dearie? Lord Exmouth will pay right 'andsomely for your safe return, I'm thinking.'

'And why should you suppose that he would be willing to do that?' Robina asked cautiously. Surely if their objective was to attain a sizeable ransom they would have been wiser to have tried to abduct the Dowager.

'Don't try those little tricks on us,' the man called Jack scoffed. 'We 'appens to know that the rich lord plans to marry you.'

So that was it! If her own position had not been so precarious, she might well have found the whole situation highly diverting. The fools had abducted the wrong female! Arabella was the one they ought to have taken, but even so, she didn't doubt for a moment that Daniel would meet these scoundrels' demands in order to attain her safe release.

Perversely, this annoyed her more than anything else. Why should he be made to part with what may well turn out to be a considerable sum of money because of her bird-witted actions? If she had not foolishly gone wandering off by herself, she wouldn't have found herself in this predicament now. Yes, she had got herself into this situation, so it was up to her to get herself out of it, she decided. But how?

She took a moment to glance at each of her captors in turn once again, her gaze lingering a fraction longer on the man with the lascivious glint in his deep set eyes.

'Well, I suspect you're right,' she conceded at last, successfully controlling her rising ire. 'Providing, of course, that I come to no harm…of any description.'

The woman at least was not slow to follow her meaning, and her full lips curled into an unpleasant smirk. 'Don't you be a'worrying none about me brother, dearie. He'll behave himself…so long as you do the same. So eat up yer food like a good girl, and we'll all leave you alone until morning.'

Robina took one glance at the unappetising broth with its film of grease floating on the top, and decided to sample just the bread, which was at least freshly baked, if slightly heavy.

'And what do you intend to do with me tomorrow, if it isn't asking too much?'

'Inquisitive little thing, ain't she?' Jack remarked to no one in particular. 'You're going to write a letter to your lord, pretty lady. And if all goes well, you'll be out of 'ere, and back in your own nice bed by tomorrow night.'

'Or in 'is lordship's,' the other man sniggered, before turning to his sister. 'I don't see why we couldn't 'ave got the thing done tonight. I told you afore, Moll, I don't like the idea of keeping 'er 'ere.'

'I don't see why,' Molly scoffed. 'No one ever comes 'ere n' more. And I can't say I blames 'em neither. You've let this place fall into rack and ruin, our Ben, since Betsy died.' Although not renowned for cleanliness herself, even Molly was appalled by the filthy state of the house. 'And as I've already told you, I ain't walking all that way back to town tonight. Tomorrow will do fine. Besides, his lordship might be more willing to part with 'is money, if he's been left to fret for a while.'

Appearing quite smugly satisfied, she turned to Robina. 'Had your fill then, dearie? That's good. We'll just let Jack 'ere bind yer hands again. No need to tie yer feet, though. I don't think you'll try to escape through the window. It's a mighty long way down.'

Robina's mind began to work rapidly as she obliged her captors by placing her hands behind her back. If she was going to effect an escape, she must make the attempt before morning. 'If—if I'm to remain incarcerated in here all night, might I not at least have a candle? It will be dark soon, and I could have sworn I saw something poke its head out of that hole in the corner earlier.'

'Ha!' Jack barked, securing the slender wrists with a merciless disregard for any pain he might be inflicting. 'Wouldn't be at all surprised if you did! The place is overrun wi' rats.' He seemed to debate within himself for a few moments. 'Don't see why she can't 'ave a candle, though. What say you, Molly?'

She merely shrugged before picking up the tray and carrying it from the room. Her brother, after one last ogling look in the direction of Robina's trim, shapely figure, followed, and then Jack went out, but came back a moment or two later with a lighted candle which he placed on the crate beside the small box bed. Without saying anything further, he went out again, the door closed, and Robina heard the bolts being securely slid into position.

Well, at least she had until morning to attempt an escape, she reminded herself, determined to think positively and not become too disheartened by her present predicament. She might be wise to wait an hour or so, or until such time as she could be sure that those three scoundrels below were asleep, which would not be too long if the odour of gin which had pervaded the room when they had entered was anything to go by. In the meantime it was only boredom with which she was forced to contend, and the pain in her wrists, where the cord rubbed against the soft flesh.

She couldn't prevent a protracted sigh escaping, as she turned to stare at the small window once more. It had grown considerably darker since the last time she had looked across at that grime-streaked single pane of glass. What time would it be now? Nine, perhaps nearer ten, she decided, and could not help wondering what had taken place with certain other persons during her long hours of incarceration.

The Dowager, poor darling, would be frantic with worry. They would have given up any search by now, of course; had possibly done so hours ago. It was possible that her ladyship had seen fit to inform the authorities, but it was much more likely that she would have returned to Brighton to apprise Daniel.

He would then have taken charge of the situation in that calm and sensible way of his. No doubt he would have informed the authorities, if his mother had not, and would have arranged for a further search to take place in the wood and surrounding area at first light. In the meantime, however…

Her eyes growing misty with tears she refused to shed, she turned her head to stare sightlessly across the dusty attic room, her mind's eye conjuring up a clear image of the library back at the house in Brighton, and of Daniel, concerned over her safety, but outwardly appearing calm and collected as always, sitting there in his favourite chair.

It would have come as something of a surprise to Robina had she known that at that precise moment, far from comfortably ensconced in his book-lined room, Daniel, his face set rigid with barely suppressed anger, was tooling his curricle at a neck-to-nothing fashion through the streets of the town in an attempt to find a certain jarvey.

Kendall, sitting on the seat beside him, cast his master a concerned glance. Never had he seen his lordship in such a rare taking—no, not even on that dreadful day, almost two years ago, when the master had ridden at the same neck-to-nothing pace along the hillside track not far from Courtney Place. Not that too many people had ever discovered that very important fact, though, Kendall reminded himself. Stebbings, he himself, and maybe one or two others knew the truth of what had happened that day when the late Lady Exmouth had died, but not one, as far as Kendall was aware, had ever betrayed the master's trust by disclosing what they had known.

'My lord,' he said in some urgency, as Daniel overtook a lumbering coach with only an inch to spare, 'are you sure you don't want me to take a turn at tooling the curricle?'

This suggestion brought a glimmer of amusement back into Daniel's eyes. 'Feeling somewhat nervous, Kendall? I thought you had more faith in my abilities. I haven't even come close to scraping the paint work, I'll have you know.'

'It isn't that,' his trusty henchman hurriedly assured him, 'as I expect you well know, sir. It's just that I ain't being of much use to you at the moment.'

Kendall was well aware of precisely why they were scouring the streets of Brighton at this time of night, and was as concerned as everyone else over Miss Perceval's surprising disappearance.

'I don't know what this jarvey looks like, sir, nor what sort of carriage he drives, neither. If I were to take over the reins for a spell, it'd leave you free to look about for the cove.'

'Thank you for the offer, Kendall, but I've already come to the conclusion that I'm on a fool's errand. It would have been wiser for me to have remained at the Crown in the hope that he might put in an appearance, or I should at least have waited for the landlord's return.' And so saying, he turned the next corner and headed back towards the tavern he had visited earlier.

'What business do you suppose can that rascally landlord be engaged in that he must leave the running of his tavern in the 'ands of his brother?'

Daniel slanted the head groom a mocking glance. 'What business do you suppose, man? He's undoubtedly acquiring fresh supplies of rum and brandy from a reliable source, if I know anything.'

'Smuggled goods, you mean, sir?'

'I wouldn't be at all surprised. There's a deal of free trading taking place all along this coast. The Preventive Officers are fighting a losing battle, and I suspect will continue to do so unless the laws are changed.'

They had by this time arrived back at the Crown. Daniel, willingly handing over the reins to Kendall now, wasted no time in alighting and re-entering the tavern, only to discover that the landlord had not yet returned. He realised at once that little would be gained in attempting to question the brother further. The man had freely admitted earlier that he helped out at the inn only rarely, and although he did know several of the locals by sight, he didn't know their names, and so couldn't say for certain whether Master Higgins had been in the inn already that evening or not.

Swiftly deciding that he had little option but to await the landlord's return in the hope that mine host was well acquainted with the jarvey, Daniel ordered himself a tankard of home-brewed ale, and had just carried it across to a corner table when the door opened and the very man he was intent on finding that night walked calmly into the inn.

His first impulse was to rush across and accost the jarvey, but he checked it. Higgins just didn't have the look about him of a man who was expecting to acquire a substantial amount of money in the very near future. In fact, he looked very sombre, thououghly dissatisfied with life. Daniel was further confounded when Higgins, waiting for his ale to be poured, looked about him, his expression registering surprise, rather than fear or uncertainty, as he glanced in Daniel's direction.

Was it possible that he had totally misjudged Master Higgins, and that the man knew nothing of Robina's disappearance? Daniel wondered. Yes, there was just that possibility, he supposed. None the less, it seemed rather too much of a coincidence that on the very next day after Higgins had foolishly proposed abducting her, she should have disappeared, he finally decided, as he watched the jarvey come smilingly across to the table.

'Why, my lord! I didn't expect to be seeing you here again. Got a taste for our local landlord's home-brewed, have you? Well, can't say as I can blame you. He serves a good drop of ale.'

'He does indeed. Why don't you join me, Master Higgins?'

The jarvey did not hesitate, which only added to the rapidly growing conviction in Daniel's mind that the man was innocent of any wrongdoing this day. But he had to be sure.

'So, what does bring you back to our neck of the woods again, my lord?' Higgins enquired, looking and sounding remarkably composed. 'Ain't the usual haunt for gentlemen of your class. Not that you can't come and go as you please o' course. And it's always nice to see a friendly face round these parts.'

Leaning back in his chair, Daniel took a moment to sample the contents of his tankard before he said, 'As a matter of fact, I came here specifically to see you, Master Higgins.'

The jarvey's surprise was too spontaneous not to be perfectly genuine. 'Me…? But why should you want to see me, m'lord?' he asked before a sudden and decidedly hopeful expression flickered over his weather-beaten features. 'You ain't been giving a bit more thought to the little suggestion I put to you t'other evening, by any chance?'

Unlike his companion's, Daniel's smile was not pleasant. 'Believe me, Master Higgins, I have thought of nought else for the past few hours.' He leaned forward, his gaze intense. 'You see, Master Higgins, Miss Perceval has indeed been abducted, or at least her mysterious disappearance bears the distinct hallmark of abduction.'

Daniel watched the stubble-covered jaw drop perceptively, as the jarvey, all astonished incredulity, gaped across the table. Either he was the most gifted actor who ever drew breath, or he was genuinely astounded. He just had to be sure which it was.

'Now, Master Higgins,' he went on, his gaze never waving for a moment. 'Very few people knew for certain that Miss Perceval would be amongst the little party spending this afternoon out at Priory Wood. The lady who organised the outing knew, as did my mother and myself… And, of course, you knew, Mr Higgins.'

The jarvey did not pretend to misunderstand. 'But—but you don't suppose I had anything to do with the girl's disappearance, do 'ee?'

'Now that is precisely what I am endeavouring to discover,' Daniel responded smoothly.

'But I swear to you on my dear Dora's life, m'lord, I've never clapped eyes on the wench—I mean, the young lady—in my life. Furthermore, I ain't left the town all day. And there's plenty who'll vouch for that an all, iffen you don't believe me.'

'I'm not suggesting that you were actively involved in Miss Perceval's disappearance, Higgins,' Daniel assured him, no longer harbouring the slightest doubt as to the man's innocence. 'What I'm trying to discover is whether you mentioned to a third party that there was to be a picnic held at Priory Wood today at which Miss Perceval was to be present?'

'Now why the devil should I go and—' The jarvey's suddenly thoughtful expression was answer enough.

'So, you did mention the fact to someone,' Daniel prompted, when his companion remained silent, staring fixedly down into the contents of his tankard.

'Well, yes. Sort of, I did, I suppose,' he admitted at length. 'And Molly Turpin's brother lives out by Priory Wood, as I remember. Took her out there some months back in me carriage when her sister-in-law passed on. Right upset she was when she discovered she hadn't been left so much as the pearl brooch she had always admired. Wouldn't surprise me none if Molly's brother hadn't sold the brooch long since and spent the money on gin,' he continued after a moment's deliberation. 'A reet bad 'un is Ben Turpin. He'd do almost anything for his gin money.'

'Even going so far as to abduct a young woman and hold her for ransom?' Daniel suggested, and Higgins looked gravely back across the table at him.

'Ain't saying he would, and I ain't saying he

wouldn't. But it seems fishy to me m'lord that after I tells Molly and that ne'er-do-well man friend of hers in this very tavern all about my visit to you, the very next day that poor lass goes missing.' He looked decidedly shamefaced. 'I wouldn't like to think that any 'arm had come to the poor girl on account of me opening me big mouth.'

Daniel refused to dwell on this very real possibility. 'Do you happen to know where I can find these people, Molly and that male friend of hers? Do they live locally?'

'Close to me own place, sir.' Suddenly galvanised, Higgins tossed the last of his ale down his throat and was on his feet in an instant. 'If you don't object, I'd like to come wi' 'ee. I know these people. I'd get more out of 'em than you could ever 'ope to, sir.'

Daniel didn't need to think twice about accepting this offer of help. Quickly returning to the curricle, he very soon found himself amidst a mish-mash of tightly packed dwellings, and began to appreciate why the man now sitting beside him on the seat would wish to grasp almost any opportunity to make some money and try to better himself. The area in which the jarvey resided was little better than a slum.

After requesting Daniel to draw up outside a

dwelling that looked shabbier than most, Higgins jumped down from the curricle and disappeared up a narrow alley, only to return a matter of minutes later looking graver than ever.

'Jack and Molly ain't there. What's more, there ain't been a sign of 'em since morning. Which ain't usual, sir. Jack Sharpe tends to do—er—most of 'is business at night, as yer might say, and spends most days 'anging round the 'ouse or in the taverns.'

'I see,' Daniel responded, having a fairly shrewd idea of precisely which profession Jack Sharpe was engaged in, and now fearing the worst. That Robina might have fallen into the hands of an unprincipled sneak-thief and his doxy filled him with dread, but, as ever, he revealed little of this inner turmoil as he added, 'I think it behoves me to pay a visit to—er— Turpin's place of residence. Do you happen to know precisely where it is located, Higgins?'

'I've been out that way only once, sir, as I mentioned earlier. But I'm certain I could find it again, even in the dark. If you like, I'll willingly come with 'ee, and show 'ee the way. Just gives me a minute to pop in 'ome and see my Dora to tell 'er I'll be working late, otherwise she'll only fret.'

After watching the jarvey slip inside a dwelling

which, from the outside, appeared in a better state than most, Daniel turned to his groom, seated on the back. 'I want you to return to the house. Inform her ladyship that I've gone out of town, and that I wish her to take no further action until I return. Which might possibly not be until morning.'

Although Kendall clambered down at once, his expression clearly betrayed unease. 'Are you sure you don't want me to come with you, sir? It sounds to me as if you might well find yourself having to deal with a right bunch of wrong uns.' He glanced briefly over his shoulder. 'And are you certain you can trust that jarvey, my lord?'

This evident concern for his safety succeeded in bringing a flicker of a smile to Daniel's lips. 'I would be the first to admit, Kendall, that where my fellow man is concerned my judgement has not always been faultless, but it has improved immeasurably in recent years. Yes, I am certain I shall not discover my trust in Master Higgins misplaced.'

By the light of the rapidly guttering candle, Robina examined the burns on her wrists. The discomfort she was being forced to endure now seemed rather a high price to pay for the removal of her bonds and the successful opening of the window. Had she been able to effect her escape by climbing down the ivy…well, that would have been a different matter entirely, but she steadfastly refused to give up hope quite yet.

In an hour or so, or when there was sufficient light to see clearly, she would consider again attempting to escape by way of the window. The ivy clinging to the house wall looked sturdy enough to support her weight, but she would be foolish not to be sure. The last thing she wished to incur now was further injury. She wouldn't get very far on a broken ankle.

Her only other option, of course, was an escape by way of the door. She glanced down at the stout piece of wood which she had managed to find under the bed, and which she had placed within easy reach upon the wooden crate. Any form of physical violence was abhorrent to her. None the less, it would not do to be faint-hearted in her present situation, she reminded herself. If the opportunity arose, she must be prepared to use that weapon, but, here again, she must wait until someone withdrew the bolts from the other side of the door. In the meantime she had at least one task to keep her occupied.

Sitting herself on the edge of the decidedly lumpy mattress once more, she tore two thin strips off her underskirt, and was in the process of binding up her left wrist when she distinctly heard a rustling noise and what sounded suspiciously like a grunt from just below the window. Then, to her horror, two large and shapely hands suddenly grasped the sill.

Stifling a scream, she darted forward. 'Who's there!' she demanded, half-fearing that it might well be the lecherous owner of the property come to pay a visit without his companions' knowledge. Reaching forward, she was seriously toying with the idea of bringing the small sash-window down hard on those two shapely, long-fingered hands when a distinctly amused and beloved voice drawled, 'Who the deuce do you suppose it is, my darling…? It is your Sir Galahad come to the rescue… Moreover, a Sir Galahad who is getting decidedly too long in the tooth for these sorts of starts.'

With a strange little sound, somewhere between a sob and a cry of pure joy, Robina almost flung herself into Daniel's arms the instant he had climbed into the room. He held her close, murmuring words of comfort, his recent exertions not wholly responsible for his rapidly increased pulse rate and erratic breathing.

'Here, let me look at you.' Reluctantly holding

her a little away from him, he ran his fingers down her arms to capture her hands, and saw the slight wince. 'What's wrong? Are you hurt?'

'It's only my wrists. I was in the process of binding them up when you arrived.' Robina could not help but smile at his muttered oath, only half suppressed, as he examined her hurts. 'I did it myself,' she assured him softly, 'when I used the candle to burn through the cord that bound my wrists.'

'So the blackguards tied you up, did they?' He certainly did not appear best pleased to learn this, but made no further comment as he reached for the second strip of material, his fingers surprisingly gentle as he began to wrap it round the injured flesh.

'How many of the rogues are we dealing with, do you know?'

'Three… Well, I've only seen three,' she amended. 'A woman and two men.'

Somewhat bemused, Robina watched him secure the bandage deftly, still not quite able to believe that he was with her. 'Daniel, how on earth did you manage to find me?'

'Now that, my little love,' he responded, smiling as he released her wrist, 'is rather a long and involved story.'

'And you'd rather not tell me now. Yes, I quite understand.'

Moving over to the window, Robina poked her head out. From what she could see, it seemed a very long way down to the ground. But this was no time to be faint-hearted, she reminded herself once again. Besides, if Daniel could manage the climb up, surely she could manage to climb down?

'Should I go first, or you?' she asked, pulling her head back to find him surprisingly shaking his head.

'Neither of us, my dear.' Daniel moved over to the door to test its strength with his shoulder. 'I'm afraid I managed to dislodge a large portion of the ivy on my upward climb. It's a miracle I made it in one piece,' he admitted with brutal frankness. 'I wouldn't care to risk a descent.'

Disappointed, but not entirely downcast, Robina looked across at the door. 'Then it would appear we'll need to resort to my second plan.'

Daniel could not help smiling at this matter-of-fact attitude. What an amazing young woman she was! Most females would have succumbed to a fit of the vapours if they had experienced half of what his darling girl had been put through this day. Abducted, tied up, and locked in a filthy attic room for hours, she appeared, apart from her dishevelled appearance and injuries to her wrists, none the worse for her ordeal.

'Evidently you have already considered an alternative means of escape.'

'Well, yes,' she admitted guardedly, 'although I haven't given much thought to how I'd actually achieve it.' She glanced down at the crate. 'But at least I managed to find myself a sort of weapon.'

'And would you honestly have been prepared to use it?' he asked, his dark brows rising sharply as he followed the direction of her gaze.

'I might have been forced to do so... Still might, if it comes to that. But at least I have until morning to think it over.'

There was no response, and Robina raised her eyes to discover him looking rather thoughtfully back across the room at her. He appeared suddenly very troubled. 'What's wrong, Daniel?'

'Nothing... Nothing at all,' he replied, but not very convincingly, before moving across to the window and surprising her further by taking a handkerchief from his pocket and waving it several times.

'Who are you signalling to?' Hope stirred. 'Is Kendall with you?'

'No, my dear. I have left my curricle and pair in the very capable hands of one Hector Higgins, about whom I shall tell you more presently. In the meantime, I would like to know whether or not you think all three of the rogues who abducted you are still in the house?'

'I believe so, but obviously I cannot be sure. I haven't heard any sounds from below for some considerable time, so I would imagine they must all be asleep…or drunk.'

'Maybe so. But I do not think we will alert them to my presence until morning.'

He evidently had his reasons, although Robina failed to see what they could possibly be. 'But what about your friend Mr Higgins? Could he not possibly alert the authorities, and tell them we're here?'

'He could, of course, but I would much prefer that he remain with the horses and await further instructions, as I've already advised him to do by my signal.' He noticed the puzzled expression. 'I am endeavouring to protect your fair name, my dear. The fewer people who know about this little escapade, the better.'

She smiled across at him, but he could easily detect the lingering puzzlement in her eyes. 'Trust me, my little bird. I have only your best interests at heart, believe me.'

Realising she was being very selfish to expect

an immediate escape, Robina decided not to press him further. He had come in search of her, putting himself at risk, and was endangering himself still further by not enlisting outside aid in order to effect her escape, simply in an attempt to protect her good name. What more could she possibly ask of him?

Suddenly finding herself unable to hold that concerned, brown-eyed gaze, she turned away, once again finding herself having to fight the threat of tears. Why, oh why had she not recognised his true worth from the first? Why had it taken her so long to appreciate that in this kindly, level-headed gentleman she had found the very man for her? Yes, she had been given her chance, and had thrown it away… And now it was all wretchedly too late!

'Well, I suppose we may as well try to make ourselves as comfortable as possible until morning.'

This very practical suggestion forced Robina to abandon her heart-rending reflections, at least for the present, and she turned to discover him testing the thin mattress, and grimacing at its lumpiness.

'Come… Come and sit beside me, and I shall tell you all about my new friend, Honest Hector

Higgins.' Daniel held out his hand, noting the slight hesitation before she obeyed.

After deliberately taking his time over the telling of the story, Daniel had the satisfaction of seeing that Robina was quite unable to keep her eyes open as she remarked in a distinctly sleepy voice, 'But what I don't quite understand is why Mr Merrell should have proposed that you abduct me in the first place.'

Smiling to himself, Daniel raised his arm and placed it about her slender shoulders so that she nestled comfortably against him. 'I think it might be wise to leave that particular explanation until morning, my love.'

Chapter Twelve

Daniel glanced across at the window. It was morning, and still he wasn't sure whether he had done the right thing by choosing to spend the night here. But it was rather too late to do anything about it now, he reminded himself, transferring his gaze to the being who had caused him hours of soul-searching.

Still lying in the crook of his arm, Robina had slept soundly throughout the night; whereas he, plagued by a guilty conscience, had hardly slept at all.

It would have been a simple matter to attempt an escape at any time throughout the night. By using another of those prearranged signals, he could have instructed Higgins to leave the horses. Using those skills acquired in his misspent youth, the jarvey could easily have broken into the house. Higgins could then have located this room, unbolted the door, and with luck they might all have walked out without any one of those villains being any the wiser. But no, Daniel reflected, he had given way to temptation and chosen not to do so.

The instant Robina, in all innocence, had mentioned she was resigned to remaining incarcerated in this room until morning, the idea that she might be persuaded to marry him if they spent the whole night together had sprung into his mind. Well, perhaps he had not behaved like a gentleman, he was forced to concede, but at least he had not sunk so low as to make a marriage between them totally unavoidable by seducing her, although that too had certainly crossed him mind. And more than just once during the past few hours, he was ashamed to say!

He could only marvel at his powers of restraint. Holding that lovely, slender body pressed against him, feeling those firm, young breasts through the thin material of his shirt had been a sweet torment, and his subsequent frustrations little more than he deserved. A judgement on him, he supposed. If it had not been for the fact that he was certain in his own mind that they would make a blissfully contented couple once they were married, he might have been able to resist this golden opportunity of at least trying to persuade her to marry him.

As though sensing his thoughts, and wishing to torment him further for the subterfuge, Robina moved her hand in a feather-light touch across his chest and down to his stomach, igniting yet again that fire in his loins.

'Steady, boy, steady,' Daniel muttered to himself, as he placed his hand over hers, instantly stilling those innocently tantalising fingers.

The brief contact of his restraining hand disturbed her. He could detect the slight movement of her eyes beneath those lids, with their ridiculously long, curling lashes which had caused such havoc with his senses when they had brushed against his chin during the night.

'It is perfectly all right, Daniel. I assure you I have them well under control,' she astounded him by unexpectedly murmuring.

'I beg you pardon, my darling?'

The delicate lids fluttered open, and she gazed smilingly up at him. 'The greys, Daniel, I...' She blinked several times as though trying to bring his features into focus, and then sat bolt upright, staring about in some confusion.

'I was dreaming we were out in the curricle.' She glanced about her again, the confused look slowly disappearing as she looked across at the window. 'Good heavens, it's morning!'

'You have been sleeping soundly in my arms all night,' some imp of mischief prompted him to tell her when she edged a little away from him.

'Good heavens!' she muttered again, looking so deliciously pink and flustered that Daniel was once again forced to exert that iron self-control and not pull her straight back into his arms. 'The last thing I remember was listening to some story about…about your acquaintance Mr Higgins.' The frown returned. 'Which, I seem to remember, didn't make very much sense, though I expect that was because I was tired and not attending properly.'

'I dare say.' Easing his aching back away from the wall, he got to his feet. 'Unfortunately I haven't the time to explain things more fully to you now, not if I stand the remotest chance of getting you safely back to the house before the whole of Brighton society starts parading the streets.'

'What time do you suppose it is now?' she asked, seeing his grimace as he flexed his arms. Little wonder he felt stiff. He must have spent the most uncomfortable night, with his back pressed against the wall, and her lying against him.

'As I left my pocket-watch, again, in Higgins's safe keeping, I can only guess, but I would imagine it must be around six.'

'In that case it is highly unlikely that our friends below have risen yet,' Robina pointed out. 'At least,' she amended, after listening intently for a moment, 'I cannot detect any sound of movement.'

'Well, they very soon will be awake.' There was a definite look of determination about him now, as he grasped the stout stick and began to pound it against the door. 'Come on, my dear, yell out. I don't wish them to be aware of my presence quite yet.'

Robina automatically did as she was bid. Taking the stick from him, she continued to hammer it against the door, shouting as loud as she could as she did so, until she detected the sound of heavy footsteps growing steadily louder.

'Now, what's all this, then? What's all this racket?' a gruff and faintly annoyed voice demanded to know from the other side of the door, and Robina was fairly certain that it was none other than Molly's obnoxious brother who had come to investigate.

She glanced briefly at Daniel, who had positioned himself in readiness against the wall so that when the door was eventually opened, he would not be seen by their visitor. She guessed what she must do next.

'Let me out of here at once, do you hear me, or I'll scream the place down!' She must have sounded as though she had meant it too, for the bolts were immediately drawn back, the door swung open, and the obnoxious owner of the neglected farmhouse stomped into the room, but not before Robina had taken the precaution of backing away a few paces, her sturdy weapon held securely in her hand.

'Who untied you!' he growled, taking a threatening step forward, and reaching out a grubby hand to grasp the stick. 'Ere, let me have that!'

'I'm afraid we are unable to oblige you. But you can certainly have this,' Daniel said suavely, thereby making his presence known, and before Ben could do much else other than swing round, startled, Daniel placed a well-aimed blow on the flabby jaw, the force of which sent Ben sprawling to the floor.

'Come, my darling, no time to waste!' Grasping a bemused Robina by the hand, Daniel whisked her from the room, sliding the bolts across the door before she realised quite what was happening. 'I'm sorry you were forced to witness that, my dear, but I'm afraid there was no other way.'

'Oh, please don't apologise, Daniel. Besides, I've witnessed you perform the feat before,' she reminded him, sudden excitement adding an extra brilliance to her eyes.

'What a redoubtable young woman you are, Robin! A veritable breath of fresh air. Which is something I hope we'll both enjoy again, once we're away from this unwholesome place.'

Feeling inordinately pleased by the surprising compliments, Robina followed him along the musty-smelling passageway to the head of a steep and narrow flight of stairs. Hampered by petticoats, she wasn't able to descend as quickly as Daniel who, having reached a second narrow passageway, began to move cautiously forward. He was halfway along its length when a door behind him opened a fraction. Before Robina could gather her wits together to scream out a warning, Molly had darted out and had jumped on his back, clawing and hissing like a cat.

It had crossed her mind to wonder whether she would have the courage to use her weapon. Now that the moment had arrived, Robina didn't need to think twice about it. Unconcerned for her own safety, she darted down the last few stairs and, raising her arm, brought the wooden stick down hard across the clinging woman's shoulders. A loud scream of pain echoed along the passageway as Molly released her grasp and dropped to the ground to land in a huddle by the wall.

There was little pity in Daniel's eyes as he glanced briefly at the hysterically sobbing female whose features were contorted in pain as she clasped her shoulder. Nor did he betray even a moment's alarm as he turned to find his way barred by the third member of the villainous gang, brandishing an evil-looking knife.

'So, you thought to free the wench, did 'ee,' Jack sneered. He didn't seem particularly interested to discover precisely who Daniel was. Evidently his only concern was that a stranger was depriving him of some easy money.

He raised the hand holding the knife. 'Well, let's see how you'd like some of this.'

'No, I don't think so,' Daniel replied, his voice silky-smooth and as soft as velvet. 'Let us see, instead, how you'd like some of this.'

Calmly delving into his jacket pocket, he did no more than draw out a pistol and discharge it before the other man had taken more than a pace or two towards him. Robina, watching the knife fall from suddenly limp fingers, couldn't decide which of Daniel's startling feats had amazed her more—his ability to floor a powerfully built man easily with a single blow, or his unerring accuracy with a pistol. She didn't suppose for a moment that he had intended to mortally wound the man called Jack, who went stumbling back along the passageway to disappear from view, merely render him incapable of foiling their escape, which he had done with precious little effort, it seemed.

'Come, my darling.' Daniel recaptured a bemused Robina's hand, as she continued to gaze up at him in dawning wonder. 'I think it's time we left this den of thieves.'

'But—but, surely we aren't just going to leave them like this,' Robina protested, as Daniel hauled her willy-nilly along the remainder of the passageway, down a second flight of stairs, and then out into blessed fresh morning air.

'I have no intention of sparing any one of them another thought,' he assured her, sounding sublimely unconcerned, as he continued to lead the way along a weed-covered path and into a narrow lane. 'None of them will suffer any lasting harm, I'm sure. They can think themselves very lucky that I'm not considering bringing charges against them.'

Robina looked up at him, uncertain whether he was being quite sensible to leave matters as they stood. She didn't consider herself a vindictive person by any means, and would be quite happy to forget the whole unfortunate experience, but she couldn't help wondering whether, having been thwarted in their attempt to make some easy money, those three incompetent abductors just might try to wreak their revenge some time in the future, and echoed her fears aloud.

'They might, of course, but I very much doubt that they will. They're not hardened criminals, merely petty thieves and, by the looks of them, not very successful ones. Besides,' he shrugged, 'I am endeavouring to ensure that your ordeal does not become widely known. Also, there is the welfare of someone else to be considered. I do not believe that I shall be troubled by those three again, but my friend Mr Higgins might not be so lucky if his part in this unfortunate business ever became common knowledge.'

Daniel continued to lead the way through a clump of trees and bushes, and eventually into a clearing beyond. 'And here he is, dutifully guarding my horses, just as he promised he would during my absence.'

Robina was delighted to make the acquaintance of the man who had made it possible for Daniel to accomplish his rescue in such fine romantic style, even if she still failed to understand why the good Mr Higgins should ever have imagined that Daniel should have wished to abduct her in the first place.

Little time was wasted in clambering into the curricle and heading back to Brighton. Thankfully at this early hour there were very few other travellers using the roads, and Robina was able to make a few necessary repairs to her appearance whilst she listened to Daniel recounting the events of the morning to his friend Mr Higgins, who had happily relinquished his seat to Robina and had climbed up on the back.

They bowled along at a sprightly pace until Daniel, quite without warning, drew the curricle to a halt. 'This is where we must part company,' he announced, turning to Higgins, who appeared as surprised as Robina by the unexpected stop as he obediently clambered down on to the road.

'In the field yonder, unless I much mistake the matter, are the first traders arriving for the horse fair. In an hour or two the place will be crowded. Take advantage of your early arrival by thoroughly examining the animals on offer before finally making your choice.'

Daniel paused to toss a bulging purse down to the jarvey. 'You'll find more than enough in there to purchase a fine animal, and to make all the necessary repairs to your carriage, if you don't choose to look round for a newer one. But before you go,' Daniel added, smiling at Higgins's expression of awestruck wonder, 'I'll thank you for the return of my pocket-watch.'

This reminder appeared to restore the jarvey's faculties. Laughingly handing up the timepiece, he offered his grateful thanks, and then set off at a brisk pace in the direction of the fair-field.

'And now that we are alone,' Daniel remarked, after giving his greys the office to start, 'there are a few little matters which we must sort out before we arrive home.'

Robina instinctively put a hand up to her hair, which she had tied back with a ribbon torn from her gown. 'I realise I must look a fright, but there's not very much else I can do.'

'Your appearance does not concern me in the least,' Daniel assured her. 'Your reputation, however, most certainly does. You have spent the whole night alone in my company. Therefore I am in honour bound to offer the protection of my name.'

A long silence, then, 'No!'

Daniel had not expected his proposal to be accepted with a great deal of gratitude or enthusiasm, and he was forced to concede that he had not expressed himself as well as he might have done, but even he was shocked by the vehemence of the refusal.

Drawing his greys to a halt once again, he turned to discover her staring straight ahead, the lines of her sweet face held rigid, as though striving to maintain her composure.

'Come, my dear. We get along together so very well.' He reached for her hand, easily retaining it in his own when she struggled to free her fingers. 'I do not perfectly understand why you are so set against marrying me,' he continued, desperately striving not to betray the deep hurt he was experiencing at this surprising show of opposition. He simply couldn't...wouldn't believe that she was so indifferent to him!

'Come, surely you can stomach me as a husband?'

'Even if I could, you don't imagine for a moment that I'd be so cruel as to steal you away from Arabella.'

Her voice had been little more than a choked whisper, and Daniel wasn't perfectly certain that he'd heard correctly. 'Arabella, did you say...? What in the world has she to do with anything?'

Robina did turn to look at him then, her expression betraying both shock and bewilderment.

'Why, everything I should imagine! She's the one you truly wish to marry.'

'Marry Arabella…?' It was Daniel's turn to look confused now. 'What in the world makes you suppose that I have any desire to marry my cousin?'

'Because I overheard you in the garden on the evening of the Maitlands' party.'

It was out before she realised what she was saying, but it was too late to do anything about it now. Daniel had digested her every word, and was now looking rather thoughtful, staring directly at her, and yet seeming to see something else.

'I don't know what you imagined you overheard, my little love,' he said at length, 'but unless I much mistake the matter that was the night I confided in Arabella, informing her that I had every intention of marrying again. Furthermore, that I had every intention of proposing that very night to the lady who had succeeded in winning my heart. She was delighted and wholeheartedly approved my choice. Unfortunately, my plans were thwarted by my future bride herself.' His tone had changed suddenly to one of gentle, teasing censure. 'Unbeknown to me, she had decided for reasons best known to herself—though I'm certain she will favour me with an explanation at some future time—to leave the party early, and has been hiding herself away and depriving me of the pleasure of seeing very much of her…up until last night, that is.'

Robina could only stare back at him in wonder. That tender look which she had so often seen in his eyes whenever he looked at her was unmistakably there again, confirming his every word. Unbelievably, he was every bit as much in love with her as she was with him, and all she could think of to say at such a moment of blissful enlightenment was simply, 'Oh.'

Daniel, however, seemed to find this precisely the right thing to say, and with great presence of mind decided to quash any lingering doubts which she might still be harbouring as to the true state of his feelings by taking her into his arms and ruthlessly kissing her.

Emerging from her first ever experience of masculine passion a little breathless, but very willing to sample a great deal more, Robina rested her head against his shoulder. 'Oh, Daniel, I've been such a fool,' she admitted, quite unable to stop those silent tears of happiness from escaping and rolling down her cheeks. 'It wasn't until I thought you wanted to marry Arabella that I realised how very much I loved you. But I never imagined for a moment that you were in love with me.' She felt that strong arm tighten about her as she inadvertently brushed his cheek with her long lashes as she peered fleetingly up at him. 'You managed to conceal your feelings very well.'

'And with good reason,' he responded, reluctantly holding her a little away so that he could look down into her face. 'Although I had decided, after our weeks in London, that you would make the perfect wife, I felt that you were being unfairly pushed into accepting an offer of marriage that you were not altogether sure you really wanted. I felt you needed more time to get to know me a little better.'

This had certainly been true, and yet now, after the heartfelt misery she had experienced during these past few days, Robina found it difficult to believe that there ever had been a time when she had experienced any reluctance in accepting an offer of marriage from him.

'I always liked you, Daniel, right from the first, and quickly grew to prefer your company to that of any other man. It was just…' She paused for a moment, unsure whether to confess her early doubts or not, and then decided that, if he was to understand her initial reluctance, only complete honesty would serve. 'It was just that I thought you could never possibly love me…any other woman, for that matter…not after…'

'Not after I had lost Clarissa,' he finished for her when her courage failed.

He glanced briefly at the slender fingers resting lightly on his sleeve, and took them gently into his own, while silently cursing himself for every kind of a fool. They were very alike in so many ways that he had instinctively known on numerous occasions precisely what she was thinking and feeling, and yet, idiot that he was, it had never once occurred to him to suppose that having to live in Clarissa's shadow was what his dear Robin had feared she must suffer if she married him.

'I should have told you the truth weeks ago, but I suppose,' he shrugged, 'the right moment just never seemed to arise. And the truth of the matter is, my darling, Clarissa hasn't entered my thoughts very often of late.'

He smiled at the frank puzzlement which sprang into blue eyes. 'Surprised…? Yes, of course you are. Because, like everyone else, you supposed I was desperately in love with my wife and utterly devastated when she died. And that is precisely what I allowed people to believe, my darling. But nothing could have been further from the truth.'

Retaining his hold on her hand, he began to rub his thumb absently back and forth across the soft white skin, as he turned his head to stare at the empty road ahead, gathering his thoughts.

'When I married Clarissa I was very young, and a trifle headstrong...arrogant, perhaps. I had been running the estate very successfully since my father's death, and felt that I was more than capable of making my own decisions, without outside interference. In many respects, I suppose, I seemed to many far older than my years—responsible, dependable. But emotionally I was not so mature. I have long since realised that I mistook infatuation for love.'

These revelations were so startling that Robina hardly knew what to say when he fell silent, as though expecting some response. 'But surely your marriage wasn't an unhappy one, Daniel?' she managed to ask, after a moment's intense thought.

'No, I wouldn't go as far as to suggest that,' he hurriedly assured her. 'It was simply that, after Lizzie was born, I was forced to face the fact that I had changed, matured, if you like, whereas my wife remained the child I had married. We simply had nothing in common. And as the years passed the differences between us became more marked, and we simply drifted further and further apart. Not to the extent that we went our separate ways, but we certainly spent less and less time together.

'I didn't object in the least when Clarissa

wished to visit London, or our house here in Brighton,' he went on to disclose. 'In fact, I actively encouraged her to do so, little realising that maybe one day she just might succumb to flattery and attention which she no longer received from me. The gentleman who had captured her interest was a certain Mr John Travers who had a maiden aunt living within easy travelling distance of Courtney Place, which of course proved mightily convenient for them both.

'You appear shocked,' he remarked, turning his head suddenly and noting the astonishment which she found impossible to conceal. 'Yes, my wife had a lover. And the truth of the matter is, my darling, I suspected as much, but chose to do absolutely nothing about it. Which is testament enough, I think, to the state of our union.

'I didn't realise to what extent my wife's feelings were engaged until I returned from London one day to find the house virtually deserted. The daughter of one of my estate worker's was being married that day, and my wife had given permission for the servants to attend the celebration. Only the butler remained in the house, and he informed me on my arrival that my wife had left the house in the company of Mr Travers an hour or so earlier to visit Mr Travers's aunt.' There was a distinctly cynical twist to his smile. 'My wife had taken to paying regular visits to the elderly lady, so I thought little of it until I learned from Kendall, who had accompanied me on my travels, that the stable-lad who normally tooled my wife's carriage was also at the wedding celebration, and Mr Travers's horse had been left in the stable. Now, that did strike me as being odd! What could be so urgent that Travers should feel the need to tool my wife's carriage himself, and not await the return of my stable-lad?'

'So you were not responsible for your wife's death at all,' Robina murmured, hardly aware that she had spoken her thoughts aloud, until he said,

'I was not tooling the carriage, no. Travers was in charge of that, and the young fool had chosen to take the hillside track, in an attempt to avoid meeting me on the road from London, I can only suppose. But I still hold myself, in part, responsible for Clarissa's death.'

'But why, Daniel?' Robina was at a loss to understand him. 'You were not even there at the time.'

There was a hint of sadness now about the smile he cast her. 'But had I been there, my darling, Clarissa would have been alive today. Had I given her more of my time, had I not been so wrapped up in my own interests, she would never have sought the attentions of John Travers.

'When Kendall and I rode out, and examined the wreckage, I realised at once that Clarissa had decided to leave me. I ordered Kendall to return to the house with my wife's baggage, so that people would merely believe that she had planned to visit Travers's aunt, although I never supposed for a moment that that had been her intention. I also instructed Kendall to say that I had arrived home before my wife had left the house and that I had been in charge of the carriage.'

'Because you didn't want the world at large to learn the truth?' Robina suggested, when he fell silent once more. 'Yes, I believe I can understand that, Daniel.'

'It wasn't so much for my sake, my darling. Although, if I'm honest, I would have to admit that my pride received a severe dent when I realised that Clarissa had grown to prefer Travers to me. But the decisions I made that day were for my daughters' benefit, rather than my own. I didn't want Clarissa's name dragged through the mud, or my children ever to discover that their mother was willing to abandon them. Everyone, including my own mother, had supposed our marriage to have been a very happy one for the most part, and I was more than willing to allow the world to continue to believe that. Only Kendall, my butler and my friend Merrell, who had travelled down from London with me that day, ever knew the truth… And now, so do you.'

'And no one will ever learn it from me,' she assured him gently, happy to think that he trusted her enough to confide in her.

'You think I didn't realise that?' The tenderness was back in his eyes as he held her close and kissed her again. 'To think that eventually I took the advice of all my friends and decided to marry again for my children's sake. I went to London to find myself a sweet, biddable girl, and found the Vicar of Abbot Quincey's daughter. Perhaps not quite such a biddable girl, as she decided that her choice of husband would be hers and not her mother's,' he said, gently teasing, 'but exactly the right girl for me.'

'I'm so very pleased that my future husband is prepared to accept me with all my faults,' she responded in an attempt to maintain this lighter mood.

'Then you'll marry me, and soon?'

'As soon as you please, my darling!' She laughed lovingly up at him. 'You see how biddable I can be when I choose.'

'Then let us hope it lasts until after the wedding.' He was suddenly serious again. 'Clarissa and I had a large wedding in London. I do not want the same for us. I should like just close family and friends to be present, and the wedding to take place in the chapel at Courtney Place, with your father conducting the ceremony, if he is agreeable.'

She approved wholeheartedly. 'That sounds simply perfect to me.'

'And soon…? You'll marry me soon?'

'As soon as ever you like,' she assured him once again.

'Then we had best not delay in making the arrangement. You may have forgotten what that gypsy woman foretold a few weeks ago, but I most certainly have not,' he announced, very reluctantly releasing his hold and turning his attention to his horses once more. 'Our first child is to be born within a twelve-month. And the way I'm feeling at the moment the prediction will very likely come true, so I think I had better return you without further delay to the protection of my mother's side.'

Robina edged herself a respectable distance away. 'Your not so biddable future bride is on this occasion in complete agreement with you, my darling.'

* * * * *